COYOTE LIES

COYOTE HUNGER BOOK 4

RHIAN CAHILL

Coyote Lies
Coyote Hunger book 4
By Rhian Cahill

For more information visit:
www.rhiancahill.com

For everyone who has waited for the rest of the story.
To Fedora who stuck with me in times where I didn't want to
stick with me.
To Tamara Y who was willing to dive in when I asked.
And for Mr.C because the person who loves you, who you love, is
all that matters. Together forever, Babe.

1

BRADY SUCKED in a breath when he rounded the bend and the first buildings came into view.

Whispering Springs.

The place he'd been born.

Eyes scanning, he eased off the gas, and took in the changes.

Here, on the outer edges of town, things looked the same. Mostly. There had definitely been changes, minor ones—new paint, some additions—but nothing stood out too much. He was sure he'd see more once he got to the middle of town but right here, on the outskirts of the town he'd grown up in, it was as though he hadn't spent over a decade living somewhere else.

A wave of comfort flowed over him.

Home.

He'd finally come home.

The years away didn't matter; in his heart he knew this was home.

Would always be home.

He'd sought out every piece of information he could before taking the job with Wild Encounters and making the journey here. The owners, Brogan Wilder and Quinn MacClellan, had intrigued him for a number of reasons. They'd managed to build a reputable company that offered wilderness adventures to shifters and humans unlike anything he'd come across in the region or the country for that matter.

Through discreet inquiries Brady also knew they were well on their way to bringing life back to an almost decimated coyote population. Both the natural packs that roamed this mountain range and the shifter pack who called Whispering Springs and surrounding mountains home.

As sovereign and regal of the Whispering Mountain coyote shifters, the two men had strengthened the pack Brady had always thought of as his in spite of not living within its midst these last thirteen years.

His chest ached, his stomach churned, bile rising up his throat, as he thought about his father's involvement in the near destruction of the once prosperous Whispering Mountain pack.

Thinking of his father always turned his insides. Brady couldn't remember much about the man from his early years, and his mother always insisted things hadn't been as bad as their final years living on the mountain, except it didn't seem to matter how much his mother said his father had once been a better man because Brady only remembered a man with a temper, a man whose anger simmered constantly and only took a small infraction—real or perceived—to set off.

Memories of the night they fled flashed through his mind.

His father's rage before he'd stormed out of the house

leaving bruises behind. His mother throwing things in bags, racing from room to room taking very few of their possessions, before finally ushering them outside. Marcus, refusing to get in the car. The fear and desperation radiating from his mother as she frantically argued with her oldest son. Her vain attempts to drag Marcus into their beat-up old truck.

From what Brady could remember, his older brother had been stubborn and had idolized their father; his refusal to leave hadn't come as a surprise, but Marcus calling their mother a traitor and a whore had.

Brady had never wanted to hurt someone as badly as he had that night. He'd wanted to punch his brother in the face until he shut up and did what their mom wanted. Especially after she'd given up and climbed behind the wheel, her gaze fixed on the road ahead, never once looking back at the son she left behind.

She'd cried the whole fourteen hours she drove. Silent tears that streamed down her face and soaked her shirt.

He had never felt more useless or terrified in his life. At fourteen he'd been too young to defend her against his brute of a father but he had succeeded in avoiding confrontations during his early teens, protecting her as best he could by not setting off his father's rage. His efforts had never been enough.

Everything had come crashing down around them the night they left. The whole world had shifted beneath his feet with one act of violence his mother couldn't ignore.

Malcolm Connelly would stop at nothing to gain sovereign.

Not even murder.

Ironic how murder had driven Brady out of the mountains and murder brought him back.

A heavy sigh left his chest; the weight of all he faced sat on his shoulders like his favorite hiking pack. A burden he had no choice but to carry. Not if he wanted to stay. And he wanted to stay.

He didn't know what kind of reception he would receive from the pack members, especially after recent events, but he hadn't expected coming home to be easy. Not after the way he and his mother had fled. With a deep breath, he straightened his spine and focused on the town that as of today would be his home once more.

Punching the accelerator, he shot forward with a little more haste than necessary and drove toward his future.

In less than a minute he was driving down the town's main street. Slowing to walking pace, he scrutinized the shops lining the road, seeing familiar stores as he headed toward the Den Cafe. The cafe had been a fundamental part of life in Whispering Springs from before Brady was born. It didn't only serve great food, it served as a meeting point, a social outing, a place for pack members to congregate, to catch up, and, for the older generation, a place to gossip.

It wasn't surprising that Brogan had suggested Brady meet him and Quinn there. He remembered them both from before he left but he wasn't sure if they remembered him. They had to have recognized his name though.

No one had mentioned who he was—or the other reason for his return to the mountains—during his interview but they knew he'd grown up in Whispering Springs. They'd spoken on the phone several times over the last few weeks and Brady felt comfortable accepting the position with their adventure company even if returning to the mountain left him with a mix of anxiety and excitement.

Funny how something he'd longed for for years could bring such conflicting emotions.

On the one hand, he couldn't wait to return to the town he loved and missed. On the other, he feared the very people he'd thought of as family for the first fourteen years of his life. *Still* thought of that way if he were honest.

The cafe came into view and Brady quickly searched the street for a parking spot. Seeing one just beyond his destination, he sped up and slipped his truck between two off-road vehicles. He set the parking brake and turned the engine off except he didn't get out.

Muscles taut and chest heavy as though a weight pressed down on it, crushing the air from his lungs, he took a moment to get himself together. After several deep breaths, Brady grunted. With determination and a small amount of self-disgust, he yanked the keys from the ignition and popped his door.

Since the night his mother took him from his home, he'd vowed to never let fear stop him. And in the last thirteen years he'd kept that promise. He wasn't about to break it now.

He'd already broken the one he'd given his mother on her deathbed. Not that he could have done otherwise. He hadn't had anything to do with his brother in over decade and even he wasn't stupid enough to think he could have changed the outcome of his brother's life by making contact sooner.

No, his brother's destiny had been set in motion all those years ago when Marcus had chosen to stay with their father instead of leaving with their mother.

With more force than warranted, Brady shoved his door wide and climbed out. Slamming it shut behind him, he locked the truck and headed for the Den Cafe.

Encountering no one on the sidewalk, he breathed in and out, slow and steady, his stride becoming more relaxed with each breath of crisp mountain air and step he took.

Only a thin layer of snow crunched beneath his boots. It had been days since the last snowfall, but it was still the middle of winter in Whispering Springs and crisp was a polite way to say the air froze your nose hairs and cracked your lungs.

The temperature might be mild today, the sky a blinding winter-blue, but it was still bone-chillingly cold.

In spite of the cold and his apprehension, Brady felt the town—his home—seeping into his bones, embracing his soul, and warming his heart.

Glancing up and down the street, he smiled.

God, it was good to be home.

Not one to hide his head in the sand, he didn't think for a second that this was anything except the calm before the storm. There would be plenty to face the minute the townspeople realized who he was. He was prepared to meet whatever they threw at him; he'd come home for good, and no matter what his brother and father had done in the past, it wouldn't stop him from being here and claiming his place in the pack of his birth.

A bell jingled above his head as he pushed through the door. The sounds of people chatting, utensils scratching on plates, hit him like a brick wall, and he smiled at the homey feel of the cafe. Stepping inside, he shut the door, blocking out the cold, and scanned the tables for Brogan and Quinn.

As his gaze passed each group, silence followed as though an invisible soundproof blanket was being laid over the room. By the time he'd located the two men he sought in a back booth, you could hear a pin drop even without the added bonus of shifter hearing.

Brady stiffened his spine and returned the smiles of the men waving him over. With deliberate steps and head high, he moved in their direction; clamping down on the anxiety eating a hole in his gut, he kept the smile on his face and his gaze on target.

He'd made it halfway across the room when it hit him.

Raw, scraping need stole the breath from his lungs and snapped every muscle in his body rigid, tore at his nerves with razor sharp edges.

What the fuck?

His groin pulsed and his cock grew hard from one heartbeat to the next. He'd left his jacket in the truck and the sweater he wore barely skimmed his hips; his jeans, old favorites, hid nothing if someone were to look. God, he hoped nobody looked.

Clenching his jaw and eyes focused straight ahead, he moved as quick as his locked muscles allowed toward the far booth and the men he'd come to meet.

Reaching the table he held out a hand to the pack's sovereign and his new boss. "Brogan."

"Brady." Brogan's grip was strong, confident. "You made good time."

"I did." Turning to the other owner of Wild Encounters and the pack's regal, Brady offered his hand again. "Quinn."

"Brady, good to have you here," Quinn said with a quick shake.

Brogan motioned for Brady to take a seat and he slid into the booth as both men took the bench seat opposite.

"Did most of the driving at night. Plus I got away earlier than I'd planned from Nebraska," he explained. "Once I made up my mind to make the move, I wanted to get here. Get started."

He jerked in his seat as another wave of lust slammed into him. His gaze skimmed the room but he couldn't pinpoint the woman who had to be here.

"Something wrong?" Quinn asked.

"Huh?" He brought his gaze back to the men across the table. "No. No. Just taking the place in. It's not all that different from the last time I was here."

Brady hoped neither man saw through his lie. Not that the place had changed, that part wasn't the lie, but he hadn't lived in a pack since leaving Whispering Springs at fourteen; he couldn't tell if they were able to sense his deception—his discomfort.

He'd been around other shifters over the years and in spite of his mother's assertions not all coyote shifters were like his father, they had never joined another pack. She hadn't left his heritage in the past though; she'd told him about every aspect of being a coyote so he knew what was happening right now even if he wasn't sure what to do about it.

Never in a million years did he think he'd find his mate the first day he came back to town.

Except coyote instincts didn't lie, and right now his were screaming his mate was right here.

In the Den Cafe.

2

JEEZ, Kat was tired. There were still hours left in the day and she was dragging her feet as though her boots were filled with concrete. Getting up at six to open the cafe hadn't bothered her until now. Then again, she was currently getting up at four and driving up to Steve McKenna's place where her sister was laid up with a busted arm.

They might be coyote shifters with quicker healing than humans but snapping the bones in your arm so they stuck out through your skin still required the help of human medical practices to repair. Besides, Gordie couldn't cook to save her life even with two arms so Kat had been going up each morning and making her and Steve breakfast, leaving pre-made lunch and dinner in their fridge too.

After today Gordie would still have to take it easy, but the cast would be off her arm. Both Steve and Gordie had protested for the last few weeks about Kat's hovering and she had to admit, if only to herself, that it had nothing to do with Gordie's busted arm or lack of cooking skills.

God. She hated thinking about what her sister had endured

at the hands of that madman. It made her equal parts murderous and sick to her stomach. Kat would have killed Marcus herself if Gordie hadn't already taken care of that.

Closing her eyes for a moment, she drew in a deep breath to calm down. She'd hold it together. Like she had for weeks now. Since the moment she'd followed her parents into the clinic and seen her sister lying in a pool of blood.

The image would never leave her. It was as though it had been etched on the inside of her eyelids. Except it wasn't a black and white image. No. It was technicolor bright and all too real, right down to the metallic stench lining her nostrils.

No one knew Kat had been inside the clinic that day because she'd had to race outside and throw up in the dumpster behind the clothing store. By the time she'd pulled herself together the place had filled with people and Gordie had been checked out and allowed to go home with Steve.

It had taken more strength than Kat thought she possessed not to follow them up the mountain. If it wasn't for Dad's promise that Gordie only had bumps and bruises, she would have. The reassurance hadn't stopped her from going without sleep for a solid week though.

She'd finally gotten that anxiety under control when Gordie had tripped on the stairs and tumbled down, snapping her arm in two. One more sight Kat couldn't erase from her memory. Along with the terror of not being able to grab her sister before she fell.

As quick as her reflexes were, they hadn't helped when she'd been too far away from Gordie when she'd tripped.

Her sister had had far too much drama in her life and Kat hoped now that Gordie had admitted and accepted her mating with Steve, all the crap was behind her. She'd do everything in her power to make sure Gordie had nothing but happy days for the rest of her life.

She figured Steve had the same goal. That man had been trying to catch her sister's attention for years. Ever since Gordie had returned to Whispering Springs to take over from their father as the pack's doctor.

Thinking of her father made Kat smile. It was good to have their parents home for a while even if the circumstances for their extended stay weren't the best. Neither of them wanted to go traveling in their RV until they were sure Gordie was settled. Which meant Kat had to put up with a few reminders about being single but she could handle those for now.

Besides, she didn't think it would be long before Steve knocked Gordie up and that would take the pressure off by giving her parents something better than Kat's single status to occupy their minds.

Smiling, she headed into the storeroom. She'd grab a box of straws and restock before the lunch crowd got crazy. Not that she needed to worry; her staff were competent and capable. In fact, with Wendy in charge of the lunch shift, they didn't need Kat getting in the way and usually she didn't. After the morning rush, she'd normally head upstairs to her apartment for a few hours before coming back down to relieve Wendy and to handle the dinner shift.

Wendy had been around for as long as Kat could remember. Granny Roe had hired the young single mom before the doors to the Den had opened and the woman had proven her worth time and time again. Especially in the years between Granny Roe's death and Kat being ready to take control of the cafe she'd received as her inheritance. And while Wendy wasn't old or not able to do the job, now that she was in charge Kat preferred to open and close the doors each day. Just like Granny Roe had done before her.

She'd been four when Granny Roe died and while Kat's memories were few, they were all fresh, bright, and happy, and as clear as though they'd happened yesterday. She fondly remembered all the times she'd been here, in the kitchen and out the front, following Granny Roe around as she'd served drinks and food, chatting with customers.

Her granny had made this place into the heart of Whispering Springs without effort. It was just the way the woman was. She welcomed everyone with a wide smile and open arms.

Kat could only hope to emulate Granny. She'd be happy if she was a fifth as welcoming and nurturing as Granny Roe had been.

Crouching down she reached for a box on the bottom shelf. Her fingers brushed the side of the box when desire exploded in her belly, snapping her upright and dropping her back on her ass. Her pussy heated, pulsed, and dampened. Her breathing hitched, quickening and shallowing to raspy gasps, and perspiration broke out on her skin; goose bumps shimmered over her body as though invisible fingers tickled her flesh.

What the fuck?

Her gaze bounced around the storeroom. Alone. She was alone.

Squeezing her eyes tight, she took a deep breath and tried to focus, tried to work out what the hell was going on.

It was there, a scent, a connection—foreign and yet... somehow familiar.

Someone I know?

No man in Whispering Springs had called to her coyote. She'd lived here all her life, not setting foot off the mountain for more than a day or two, never wanting to. Kat swallowed, a dry mouth and constricted throat making it difficult. Chills raced up and down her spine in spite of the heat blazing inside her.

Her head cocked to one side as a shiver of knowledge rolled through her. He knew she was here; she could feel him searching for her—his coyote reaching for hers. She jerked, muscles quivering with tension while her coyote tugged to be free.

She couldn't place who had her coyote clawing for release. Didn't readily recognize the scent or connection.

A stranger?

Another wave of heat and need rolled through her making her moan.

God. This couldn't be happening. She was sure she didn't know who had her inner animal wanting to burst free so she could roll over and submit. It had to be a stranger despite of the familiarity she felt.

A stranger in town wasn't necessarily a bad thing except she wasn't about to welcome her mate with open arms. Not until she knew who he was. Even then, mate or not, Kathren Joy Monroe would not allow her inner animal to dictate who she spent the rest of her life with. She was in charge of her own future and she wasn't about to let some *mate* change where she saw it going.

Shaking herself, Kat bent forward to retrieve the box of straws she'd come in for. There was no use putting it off, she'd just march out into the restaurant and see who her supposed mate was. Only when she pushed to her feet her legs wouldn't work properly, her knees shook, and when she left the storeroom she wobbled like she had after she'd shifted the first time.

Frustrated at her lack of control, she tossed the box on the countertop and leaned against the kitchen wall. She prided herself on her self-control and to lose it so quickly annoyed and angered her.

The anger was good. She could work with that, channel it and focus it on the problem. Clenching her fists she straightened her spine and steeled her resolve.

Nothing and no one made Kat's decisions for her, including her coyote half.

Gordie said she was a control freak but Kat just liked to make her own choices—decide her own path. She had a clear goal when it came to her life, and she was well on her way to achieving it; there was no way she would let some stranger—her supposed *mate*—derail her because their animals were meant to be together.

Fucking stupid fated-mate bullshit.

For the first time in her life she cursed her coyote genes.

"Hey, boss, you all right?"

Wendy's question broke Kat from her thoughts. Turning her head, she saw the older woman carrying a huge tray of dirty dishes just inside the door leading to the dining area.

Forcing a smile, she pushed off the wall. "Yeah, taking a moment to catch my breath. I've been run off my feet all day and that day started well before dawn."

"You still checking in with your sister each morning before work?" Wendy's voice was laced with concern, her forehead wrinkled in a frown as she made her way across the kitchen. "I can't believe she snapped her arm in half walking down a flight of stairs."

Kat couldn't either. Gordie had fought off a madman and come away with barely a scratch, then she'd slipped at the top of the stairs in the house she shared with her new husband, Steve, and tumbled to the bottom. Kat shook her head. Her sister had come out of that incident with a busted arm, a concussion, and a huge dose of embarrassment.

"Today was the last day. She got the cast off this morning so she'll be able to drive from now on. Not that she hasn't tried to already." Kat scowled, a grumble of displeasure leaving her throat at the thought of her sister attempting the treacherous snow-covered mountain roads with a cast on her arm.

Wendy laughed as she laid the heavy tray on the counter by the sink and opened the dishwasher. "Why does that not surprise me? Honestly, you Monroe women are all alike. Never let anything stop you from doing what you want. Stubborn to the core the lot of you," Wendy said as she glanced over her shoulder at Kat, her twinkling eyes and smile showing her words weren't meant as an insult.

Kat grinned. Wendy was right, although Kat preferred the word determined. Her friend's observations reminded her she didn't have to let the appearance of her *mate* interfere with her life.

Monroe females were independent, capable women who did what they set out to do, and they didn't need a man to get it done. She needed to remember that and continue to take her own path as Granny Roe, her mother, and sister had before her.

"I like to think we're determined." Kat walked over and reached for a stack of bowls. "And capable. There isn't anything a Monroe woman can't do."

"Being capable and determined doesn't mean you shouldn't accept help, young lady. There's greater strength in accepting help than there is in doing it alone. Take this place. You couldn't do it without all of us."

Kat's gaze jumped to Wendy's. "That's different."

Wendy shook her head. "No, it isn't, but I'm not arguing with you about it. We've got a full restaurant out there. Let's get this load in and started before we run out of clean plates."

In silence they packed the dishwasher and when the last plate was in Wendy closed the door and hit start.

"Right. Back to the trenches. Where you don't need me because you're capable but I'm helping anyway," Wendy said with a wink before striding across the room and slipping through the door to the restaurant.

Kat shook her head and pondered Wendy's words. The older woman made sense except Kat didn't think it applied to her current situation at all. Running the Den had nothing in common with finding your mate. It was two completely different things. This was a business. A mate was for life. She already had her life mapped out and nowhere on there was a mate mentioned.

Bracing herself, she followed Wendy's path and pushed through the swinging doors.

Time to face this new hurdle to the future she'd mapped out for herself and find a way over, under, around, or through it—*him*.

3

BRADY'S WHOLE BODY TENSED. Like a bowstring pulled tight ready to snap free when the arrow was released, every muscle strained to its breaking point.

Fuck.

He hadn't been prepared for this. His mother had told him what to expect when he met his mate, but *fuck*, this was way more than his imagination had conjured up.

Whoever his mate was, she moved closer. And closer.

His skin itched and his coyote howled, and it took everything he had not to shift in the middle of the cafe. With his hands clenched around the edge of his seat, he could only hope his claws didn't rip the material to shreds. He had to grind his back teeth to smother the growl rumbling up his throat and hold the shift at bay.

"You all right?" Quinn asked, a slight smirk tipping up one side of his mouth.

Nodding, Brady stretched his lips into what he hoped was a reassuring smile.

"Oh, hey, Kat, come over here and meet our newest Wild Encounters employee." Brogan waved at someone behind Brady.

Someone Brady was one hundred percent certain was his mate.

The sovereign's smile held genuine affection and Brady's coyote growled. He didn't like another man smiling at his mate. Knowing it was inevitable, Brady braced himself and turned to look at the woman Brogan waved over.

He grunted at the slam to his gut. He'd heard people talk about a metaphorical gut-punch but he'd never experienced it before and this was a one-two deal because *fuck,* he knew her. His mate.

Ren.

Jesus fucking Christ, it was *Ren.*

Brady hadn't seen her in thirteen years. Thirteen years of wondering what she was doing, what she looked like now, whether she would remember him...

"You!" Her arm shot out, finger pointed.

Okay, she remembered him.

"Get out!" That arm swung toward the door.

"Ah—" He glanced at Brogan before bringing his eyes back to Ren.

"Your kind isn't welcome here!" she yelled.

His kind? Coyote or Connelly? "Ren."

"Kat!"

The snap of authority had Brady jolting and Ren halting in her tracks. Brady pulled his gaze from Ren to find Brogan had risen to his feet, a scowl on his face that would cower the strongest of men. Only Ren didn't back down. If anything she straightened her spine and tipped her chin up.

"He's not welcome in my cafe." She crossed her arms, her

defiant stand broadcasting loud and clear how she felt about him. The fact she was willing to go up against the pack sovereign said a lot about her dislike.

"It's okay." Brady got to his feet. "I should—"

"No." Brogan raised his arm, blocking Brady's way. "Kat, I understand this is difficult for you, but Brady has as much right to be here as any member of our pack."

She flinched, her gaze dropping slightly, but her anger didn't subside; she vibrated with it. "This is my business. I say who can and can't come in here. He can't."

Brogan sighed. "Kat."

"*My* business," Ren repeated.

"Fine. We'll take our meeting elsewhere." Brogan turned to Quinn. "Call Dale; we'll use the conference room at the station."

"Kathren Joy Monroe, you apologize to that young man right now."

Brady watched Ren's eyes close as she sucked in a breath, and the spectacular set of boobs she hadn't had last time he'd seen her thrust forward making his cock pulse, his coyote growl.

"Dad."

"Don't you *dad* me."

Brady looked beyond Ren to see Doc Monroe a few feet away, hands on hips. "It's okay, Doc," he reassured the older man. "I can—"

"No, it is not. There's no call for this kind of behavior. Kathren?"

"He's not welcome here," she said, a stubborn tilt to her chin as she spun to face her father.

"Here? On the mountain, in the town where he was born?" Doc took a step closer but didn't bother to lower his voice. Everyone in the room would hear him even if he whispered.

"You weren't raised this way. Don't let your anger taint another with someone else's sins."

"Goddammit." Kat spun on her heel once more only this time she headed across the room to the door leading to the kitchen, calling over her shoulder, "Fine. But I don't have to be in the same room as *him*." She spat out the word 'him' as though it tasted foul on her tongue.

Brady's lips twitched with the urge to smile. He remembered Ren being full of blunt honesty. It was one of the things he'd liked most about her when they were kids. There were plenty of other reasons to like Ren Monroe—then and now if the curve of her ass and sway of her hips was any indication. Of course that could be because his mate was definitely in the cafe.

She fucking *owned* the place.

"I'm sorry, son." Doc Monroe's voice dragged his gaze off Ren's retreating ass. "It's been a rough few weeks. Still, that's no excuse for Kat's behavior."

"Why do you call her Kat?" Brady asked. "She was always Ren."

"She was..." Doc Monroe frowned, deep furrows forming on his brow and either side of his mouth. "That changed after you left."

Brady didn't know what to make of that. He had been the one to nickname her Ren when they were toddlers, unable to get his tongue around Kathren he'd shortened it. They'd spent so much time together over the years. His mother had been Doc Monroe's office manager and she'd taken care of Brady, his brother, Ren, and her sister, whenever they weren't in school while doing her job.

Shaking himself from the past, he held out his hand. "It's been a while. It's good to see a familiar face."

"I bet it is." Doc shook his hand, his other cupping their

joined hands in a warm clasp that had Brady's hope for a smooth transition back into the pack growing. "When you're ready, come by the clinic and we'll deal with a few things so you can get settled at home without all that hanging over your head."

"Thank you. I'll head your way as soon as I finish with Brogan and Quinn."

"We're done, Brady. You're hired, all your paperwork is filed, you have the office address, the spring schedule, and a start date. We weren't planning on an official meeting, more a welcome to Wild Encounters lunch," Brogan explained.

"Oh."

Quinn laughed. "I'm not sure I'd eat here if I were you though." With a glance toward the kitchen, the regal murmured, "Who knows what Kat is up to back there."

"She'd better be putting the finishing touches on my lunch. Don't worry, Brady, she always packs too much, you won't go hungry." The older man patted his back. "Why don't you head on outside and wait for me? We'll walk across to the clinic together."

"Okay, sir. Thank you." Brady looked at Brogan. "Are you sure we've got everything sorted out?"

Nodding, Brogan said, "Yes. And don't worry about Kat. She'll come round."

Brady didn't think she'd be coming around any time soon. From what he knew, his brother had tried to kill her sister. He'd be lucky if Ren got over that by the time he was a hundred.

He shook hands with Brogan and Quinn, telling them to call if they needed anything between now and his first day of work. Making his way outside, he ignored the quiet that had fallen over the cafe during the confrontation with Ren.

Out on the sidewalk, he took a deep breath and once again

studied the changes to downtown. Across the street the clinic and the clothing store appeared to have had facelifts. The bookshop on the other side of the clothes shop was new. He might duck in there before heading out to the house.

The house that was now his, according to the lawyer who'd called after Marcus's death. Brady could only assume their father had left the house they'd grown up in to Marcus because it was the same address.

He thought about the packet of information the lawyer had overnighted the first week of January. All Brady had been able to bring himself to do was read the letter from the lawyer. He'd have to deal with all the other papers eventually. According to his brother's lawyer, there was nothing pressing.

His gaze returned to the clinic across the street. Nothing pressing except dealing with his brother's body.

Before he could go down that dark road of thought, the door behind him opened and Doc Monroe came out carrying a bag of delicious smelling food.

"Come on, son, let's go tuck into this hearty lunch before we have to deal with the unpleasant stuff. No point spoiling our appetites."

If whatever was in the bag tasted as good as it smelled, Brady would work twice as hard to get Ren to forgive him. "Lead the way."

"I'll warn you in advance. Gordana is at the clinic today."

Brady's step hitched and he stumbled off the curb. "Is that going to be a problem?"

"Not for me. Not for Gordana either." Doc Monroe shook his head. "You aren't to blame for what your brother or father did, Brady."

He took the squeeze Doc Monroe gave his shoulder as a supportive gesture and soaked in the comfort of knowing this man and the woman his brother had tried to kill didn't hold a grudge. It was a shame Ren didn't follow their lead.

"I'm not sure what I'm supposed to do with Marcus," he mumbled as they crossed the street.

"You don't have to make a rush decision on that. We can continue to hold his body for as long as you need."

"That doesn't seem fair. Or right. Not after..." Slowing on the sidewalk in front of the clinic, Brady attempted to communicate his feelings. "You shouldn't have to deal with this at all."

"Not much choice. We deal with the dead as well as the living as the only two doctors in town. Life is full of unpleasantness that we must work our way through."

"But—"

"No buts." Doc Monroe opened the door to the clinic. "It is what it is, and we do what we have to when we have to."

Brady grabbed the door, held it open, and waved Doc Monroe in ahead of him. "Thank you. I'm still going to make this as painless for everyone as possible."

"Dad? That you?" The woman's voice could only belong to Gordana Monroe, and Brady took a deep breath and stopped just inside the reception area.

"Yep. I've got lunch and a visitor." Doc Monroe continued across the room toward the hallway that Brady assumed led to the back of the clinic.

The place had been renovated while he'd been gone. The reception desk now sat to the left instead of the right and the way to the exam rooms sat directly opposite the front door. To his right was an area filled with kids' toys and a small bookshelf loaded with books. Above that, on a wall mount, hung a flat-screen TV currently playing a cartoon.

Back when his mother ran the office, there had been a smaller children's area she'd made in one corner of the room where the reception desk now took up space. Gone was the timber wall paneling; in its place a coat of bright, crisp white paint and a couple of colorful posters with letters and numbers in the kids' area but otherwise the walls remained bare.

Strangely it didn't feel sterile and cold like other doctors' offices. He couldn't remember if it had in the past but he liked the welcoming feeling this room gave him.

"Brady?"

"Huh?" He stopped his study of the room and met Doc Monroe's gaze. "I like what you've done with the place."

"You can thank Gordana for that. When she took over, she spruced up the place and rearranged a few things, giving us a dedicated exam room for children. I have to admit, she's improved the place even when it was already functional and worked well enough. C'mon, let's take this food into the break room and chow down before it goes cold."

Following Doc Monroe, he entered the hallway as a woman stepped out of a room at the other end. Brady stopped. He hadn't seen Ren's sister in longer than he'd been gone but he'd recognize her anywhere. In spite of them only sharing a mother, the Monroe girls looked a lot alike.

Sucking in a breath, he let it out slowly before saying, "Hello, Gordie."

Her head snapped up from the sheet of paper she was studying, her gaze connecting with his. "Brady?" Her eyes widened before a smile stretched across her face. "Oh my god! Brady Connelly!"

He wasn't prepared for the warmth in her greeting and he definitely wasn't prepared for her to race down the corridor and launch herself into his arms.

Squeezing him tight, she said, "It's so good to see you."

Returning her hug and closing his eyes, he muttered, "It's really good to see you too."

And he meant it. The thought of his brother succeeding in

hurting this woman had him shuddering. The fact she'd hurt—killed—Marcus didn't cause him a flicker of animosity or anger. All he felt while he held Gordana Monroe close was relief.

Relief that his brother hadn't damaged this woman. It remained to be seen how much his brother and father had damaged the Whispering Mountain pack and Brady's chance of being accepted back into the fold.

4

BRADY SLOWED down when he came to the turn that was familiar but not.

The trees along the drive had grown taller, their canopies thicker, and newer, smaller trees sprouted out of the ground between them. He couldn't tell if the flowers his mother had planted at the sides of the property entrance were still alive under the layer of snow covering everything or if the forest had reclaimed the flowerbeds she'd spent so much time tending.

One thing he could tell was the neglect of the driveway. Even with the snow he could see tall grass grew on what was once a gravel track. He'd have to fix that. It shouldn't be too hard but he'd need to wait until spring to do a proper job.

Having four-wheel drive helped navigate what amounted to off-road conditions but he still brought the truck to a crawl as he bumped along. Inch by inch he made his way toward the house he'd always thought of as home.

Even when it had resembled a war zone.

It had been all he'd known for his first fourteen years. Strange how almost as many years away couldn't change that deep sense of connection. The home Hank had given Brady and his mother had been a sanctuary compared to the house he slowly made his way toward and yet, this one would always be home in his heart.

Excitement and trepidation mixed together to make his nerves dance, his chest tighten.

He expected to find the place rundown, especially since no one had lived here for weeks, and he had no idea if his father or Marcus had looked after the place over the years. Throw in the storm that had swept across the mountain Christmas Day and he wouldn't be surprised to find snow had caved the roof in, and no doubt the pipes would be frozen.

Power would be an issue too. He had planned for the possibility of camping out. Good thing he didn't mind the cold and he'd come well equipped for both the freezing temperatures and being out in the open.

The back of his truck was packed with gear. He had everything he needed to spend a night or more outdoors. He would have to figure out what repairs he needed to do fast though. They were due to get another round of snowstorms next week.

Roof and pipes would be first. Windows, doors, walls. Probably should put a generator on that list too. He didn't think the one here would still run. Lots of work to do before spring arrived.

Two months.

Roughly two months to get his life in order before he took his first set of adventurers into the mountains. Brogan and Quinn shut their operation down through the winter months but everything fired up again the last week in March. Day treks, overnighters, and the longer camping trips happened March through October.

Brady had jumped at the chance to work at Wild Encounters. He'd heard a bit about them from people he'd guided at his old job. It wasn't until his mother had died last year that he'd even entertained the idea of coming home. But when he'd heard of the job opening and that his father was no longer sovereign, he couldn't apply fast enough.

He'd accepted the position only days before he received the call about his brother.

The news hadn't changed Brady's desire to come home. If anything, it had grown greater—more urgent.

There were so many ghosts that needed to be put to rest. Discovering his father's body lay in the cold-storage unit alongside Marcus had been a shock. He hadn't felt anything either way about the demise of the man who'd raised him. Probably because Malcolm Connelly had very little hand in making Brady the man he was. That had been all his mother's doing. And the man she'd sought refuge with all those years ago.

Brady smiled when he thought of Hank. He'd never met the man before that day, but the relief coming off his mother when they arrived on Hank's doorstep had been obvious. He knew they'd found someone they could trust.

Hank, according to Brady's mother, was an old friend. It took a few years for Brady to fully figure out what kind of old friend Hank was.

They'd been lovers before. And after.

In the years following their arrival, Hank had proven time and time again his love for Brady's mother as well as Brady. If he were honest, Brady would admit to wishing more than once that Hank *was* his father, that they'd always lived on the farm in Nebraska.

When Hank died in a freak accident out in the fields, Brady had felt as though part of himself had been ripped away. To say his mother had been devastated was understating it. She'd curled in on herself and left the work she'd once shared and enjoyed with Hank to their employees.

Brady still couldn't believe how much Hank's place was worth or that he'd left it all to him and his mom.

Things had been different after the accident; his mother barely talked, never smiled, and as her health deteriorated, Brady knew he'd be saying goodbye to her soon. On her death bed, she'd made him promise to find his brother. Make peace with Marcus.

He still wasn't sure what she'd hoped to achieve by extracting that promise but it was too late now to keep it. Then again, he stared through the windshield as his childhood home came into view; maybe he could find peace for himself. Put some ghosts to rest and make a future here, in the house where he'd been born.

Surprise filled him when he pulled up in front of the house. The place wasn't nearly as rundown as he expected. If he didn't know better, he'd think someone still lived here. Except there was no smoke coming from either of the chimneys and if someone was here they'd have at least one fire roaring to warm the place up.

Turning off the truck, Brady climbed out and looked around. Other than the layer of snow covering everything, the whole area had a lived-in feeling. He supposed it had been lived in until a few weeks ago. From what Sheriff Turner had told him in their one brief phone call, Marcus had been here, teaching at the high school, until early December when he'd kidnapped the sovereign's mate and been exiled from the pack.

Brady didn't have all the information on that yet, but he planned to meet with the sheriff and find out exactly what had happened. He'd thought about asking the sovereign except Brogan was his boss and that didn't seem like the right thing to do this early in his new employment. He wanted to keep those areas of his life separate for now. They were bound to mix eventually but he wanted to make sure nothing got tangled in a way that could affect either his job or his place within the pack.

With a deep breath, Brady shook off his thoughts and moved toward the house. Shin-deep snow made the walk slow; not knowing what might lie beneath that layer of white slowed him further.

He paused at the bottom of the steps. It wasn't anxiety he felt, more a buzz of anticipation. These next steps were the first of his future.

Coming home had been the plan. Finding his mate here, in the mountains he'd spent years yearning for, to find she was someone he'd loved as a kid...

Ren.

Memories bombarded him.

She'd been his best friend—his everything—when they were younger. He'd let her boss him around, let her lead him into trouble. Now that he'd seen her again, he couldn't fathom how he'd survived all these years without her.

It had cut him deep to leave and not look back, not try to contact her. The one time he had tried, his mother had nearly had a heart attack and made him promise to never do it again. Told him to forget about everything and everyone to do with Whispering Springs.

He'd tried to follow her wishes. He really had. Except forgetting Ren had been impossible and now he knew why. They might have been too young to understand their connection in their youth but they were both well aware of what it meant now.

The question was what they'd do about it.

She hated him.

He couldn't blame her.

Except...he couldn't accept that. Wouldn't. If it took him

every breath until the day he died, Brady would work to change her mind.

He'd give her every reason to love him again.

But first he had a house to check and a list to make.

He bounded up the front steps and it wasn't until he reached the top that he thought about what a foolish move that was. The house might look lived it but that didn't mean it was sound. He could have broken a leg if one of the steps had given way under his weight.

With a little more care, Brady crossed the small porch and reached for the door. He wasn't sure why he expected it to be unlocked but he twisted the handle and pushed the door open anyway.

Frowning, he eyed the mechanism and realized it was a simple door handle without a lock at all. The back of the door didn't reveal a deadbolt either so there was no way of locking the front door. A glance down revealed something more unexpected. A metal plate with a hole at one side covered the threshold.

Brady stepped inside and pushed the door closed to inspect it more closely. What he discovered confused him a little. No deadbolt but there were two heavy duty slide bolts with padlocks. One at the bottom of the door that corresponded with the plate at his feet and another bolt at the top that fitted into a solid steel bar that spanned the doorframe.

A thought struck him and he opened the door again to recheck the outside. Frowning, he wondered how Marcus had locked the front door when he left the house. The only way to lock it was from the inside. And why would his brother need such heavy duty locks?

The door was the least of his worries though, and he headed into the living room to see what condition it was in. The fireplace was stacked ready for a match so he assumed the chimney was clear but he'd take a look when he climbed onto the roof to be sure.

Each room proved the same. While the furnishings were old and a little worse for wear, they'd do for now. Every window was nailed shut prompting more questions he didn't have a clue how to answer, and there was even some non-perishable food in the small pantry in the kitchen.

After living in the huge farm house Hank owned, Brady had some ideas of what he wanted to do with this place to improve it. First he needed to make sure the roof wouldn't collapse on his head.

Back in the kitchen he discovered where the deadbolt was. Marcus must have been coming and going through the back-door, not the front. Although there was another set of steel bars and slide bolts with padlocks there as well.

Nailed shut windows, padlocked doors...

What the hell had Marcus been up to?

The answer to that question might not be something Brady wanted to know. Maybe the sheriff could give him a few answers.

He found the shed locked tight with yet another set of steel bars and padlocked slide bolts. He'd need to see about getting the keys or cutting them off. Catching sight of a ladder half buried beneath the snow alongside the shed, he dragged it out, and shouldering one end, continued to drag it through the snow to the back of the house where the roof was lowest.

Steadying the thing took time because he had to dig out snow to find solid ground but once he did, he was up the ladder and on the roof. He kicked snow off with his boot to see what condition the tiles were in.

"Damn." He gazed over the slope. "It's a fucking brand new roof?"

Down on his knees, Brady scraped away more snow and found the same thing. New shingles.

Marcus must have replaced it recently. His brother might not have updated any of the furniture or appliances but he'd made sure the roof held up. Which meant the chimneys were probably clear. Just in case an animal had found its way into one, Brady climbed to each and used the flashlight on his phone to check.

He wasn't a chimney sweep but he was smart enough to work out no animals had found homes inside them. Rubbing his cold hands together, he thought about starting the fire in the living room so he could defrost, then he remembered he needed to check the pipes and see if the old generator still worked.

It was going to be a long afternoon being wet and cold.

5

JANUARY 19

"HE'S THE REASON, isn't he?"

Kat swung away from the filing cabinet to find her sister standing inside the small office in the back of the Den. "What?"

"Brady. He's the reason you never followed through on all the talk about being a lawyer, about getting off the mountain?"

Sighing, Kat shook her head. "No. Not even close."

"But—"

"I never wanted to leave the mountain."

Gordie tilted her head, studied Kat as though she'd smeared her on one of those medical slides she was so fond of and pushed it under a microscope. "You're going to have to explain that to me. You never talked about staying here. Taking over the Den."

Kat laughed but there was no humor in it. "How could I? Why would I? What would you all have said if I'd voiced what I wanted? Jeez, you and Dad are doctors, Mom's a nurse. I barely made it out of high school and would have quit sooner if Mom and Dad had let me."

"What's that got to do with anything?"

"You wouldn't understand. All you ever wanted was to get away."

"No. All I ever wanted was to fit in!"

Kat eyed her sister. "Is that why you mated Anthony? To fit in?" God. How had she missed that?

Anthony had been an outsider who'd only lived in Whispering Springs a couple of years when Gordie accepted his mate claim.

Gordie glanced away. "We wanted the same thing."

God. So much of her sister's past began to make sense. "To belong."

"Yeah."

"But you did. You were, *are*, my sister. How could you think you didn't fit? I worshiped you. To the point I ignored what I wanted and said I wanted what you told me I should."

"What?"

Laughing, Kat asked, "You don't remember?" At Gordie's head shake she continued, "Jeez. We were arguing over something, I can't even remember what or when, and you said that I should be a lawyer. I would make a great lawyer because I could argue under water even when I was wrong."

"And you went with that? Jesus, Kat, you were born a nurturer. Running the Den fits you. Every time I see you I'm reminded of Granny Roe. The way you both always feed people, check they're okay. You might be bossy with it but your heart is behind it. I don't think you've met anyone you didn't want to *mother*, didn't love in some way."

"Love is not what I feel for the Connellys."

"Malcolm and Marcus."

"What?"

"It was Malcolm and Marcus. You can't tar Brady with the same brush, Kat. He was just a kid when he left here."

"He's one of them."

Gordie sighed and shook her head. "No. He was never like them; even as a kid he was different, and he hasn't been here for over a decade. Whatever it is you've got going on in your head about him, it's has nothing to do with what his father and brother did." Gordie moved closer, put her hand on Kat's arm. "What did Brady do, Kat?"

Kat's spine snapped straight. Was she so easy to read? "He's a Connelly."

"Yes. He is. But he's not the Connelly who tried to kill me. Or the one who tried to run Quinn down. Or the one who turned humans against their will and left them to suffer. Or the one who terrorized Rowen. Kidnapped El. Those and many more deeds were perpetrated by either Marcus or Malcolm Connelly. So tell me Kat. What has *Brady* ever done to us?"

"He left! Without a word. Up and gone when he'd promised!"

"Promised what?" Gordie prodded.

Sighing, Kat muttered, "He'd always be my friend. Always be there."

"When? When did he promise you that?"

"The year before he left."

"So when he was a kid, when he had no control over his life or what happened. Don't you think you owe him the opportunity to explain? Don't you want to know why he left, why he didn't come back until now?"

"No!" She yanked her arm out of her sister's grasp. "I don't care. He *lied* to me!"

Gordie grabbed her shoulders and shook her. "Stop. Stop thinking with a teenager's pain and think. Think about why, what could have made his mother pack up and leave in the middle of the night. Think about what Malcolm Connelly did to this pack while he was sovereign. Think about the things Marcus did, when he was a kid and when he was an adult. Think about those things, then think about what it must have been like to live with those two men. *Think, Kat.*" Gordie gave her another shake, harder enough to clack her teeth this time. "Think about what happened the day you asked Marcus about his brother."

Oh god.

She hadn't thought about that day in years. Brady had been gone nearly two years when she'd run into Marcus outside the cafe. She'd asked him about his brother and when he hadn't answered her, tried to brush past, she'd grabbed his arm and begged him to tell her where Brady was.

Unaware of the senior Connelly coming up behind her, she'd peppered Marcus with questions. He'd remained silent and only when his gaze drifted behind her did she turn and find an angry Malcolm staring down at her.

The sovereign had yanked her hand from Marcus's arm and bent over until his face was right in hers, his hand squeezing her forearm so hard she thought he'd break it, and yelled at her to never mention that name again.

There were more words spewed about betrayal, desertion, running away like a coward, but to this day Kat couldn't remember all that Malcolm Connelly had said because the pain in her arm had been too great. Her brain had screamed in agony, the internal screech ringing in her ears until she heard nothing else.

It was only when William Brant happened by that the sovereign let go and stepped back with a smile on his face. She definitely remembered his next words.

You be careful now, Kathren; a half-blood like yourself wouldn't want to have an accident like your sister.

It hadn't been a direct threat but the implication was there all the same. It was in his eyes too. Dark, evil eyes that made her skin crawl, made her shrink away in fear.

She hadn't said a word to anyone before sprinting away. She'd headed straight home and hadn't told anyone about it until Gordie had asked about the bruises on her arm. Swearing her sister to secrecy, she'd hidden the bruising under long sleeves until there wasn't a trace of them and never mentioned the incident again.

In fact, she'd all but wiped it from her mind.

"He's not to blame, Kat. You owe him an apology," Gordie said softly.

Kat took her sister's words for what they were. A suggestion as well as a reprimand. "I wouldn't go that far," she muttered.

"Well, maybe you could do something that would be a peace offering at least."

"Like what?"

"He's been out at the Connelly house for days. No one has seen him or heard from him and you know as well as I do if he'd been in town, you'd have heard about it at the Den from those old gossips."

"Maybe he left." Kat wasn't sure why that thought made her chest hurt and her coyote howl. Okay, fine, she knew.

Gordie arched one eyebrow but remained quiet.

"Fine. I'll see about getting some meals organized for him. I'm sure he's got work to do on the house and he's a guy so he probably can't cook anyway. He'll starve to death or freeze to death if he's left alone out there for too long."

Gordie's smile held a secret knowledge that Kat wasn't privy to.

"What? What's that smile?"

"Oh nothing. Be sure to tell him there's no rush on deciding what to do with the bodies."

"Bodies?" Kat thrust a hand up to stop her sister's reply as soon as her brain clicked. "Don't say it."

"It doesn't hurt me to say their names."

"No, but it will remind *me* and I don't need any more reminders than my memories, thanks."

"Are you ever going to admit you saw me?"

Kat's gaze locked with Gordie's. "How...?"

"Steve saw you. He told me because he thinks your constant hovering is because you're not dealing with seeing me covered in blood and thinking the worst."

"I'm dealing."

"No. You're coping."

Kat shrugged. "Same thing."

"No. It's not." Gordie reached for Kat's hand. "I'm here to talk any time you want."

"You don't need to talk about it."

"I don't now, but I did. And more importantly, I need you to know I've come to terms with what I did, Kat. I want you to accept it too."

"Accept it? Jesus, Gordie, I'd have killed him if you hadn't. The only regret I have is that *you* had to do it."

Smiling, Gordie murmured, "You sound like Steve."

"We both know you and love you, and with everything you believe in, we understand that taking a life isn't something you'd ever want to do." Unlike her. Kat still wanted to kill Marcus. If she could raise the dead she would, just so she could kill him all over again.

"No, I'd never want to but I'm comfortable with the fact I had to."

"Comfortable?"

"It was the right decision. For me and for the pack. If I had to live it again, I'd do it exactly the same."

"You would?" Kat studied her sister. Tried to gauge the truth in Gordie's words. She couldn't find any sign of a lie.

"In a heartbeat. And if I'm honest, I'd have to admit I'd tell everyone about the attack in the mountains all those months before, and all the little things that were happening at the clinic and the house, about my suspicions; I wouldn't keep those to myself so I guess I would do some of it differently."

"I was so angry with you when I found out you'd hidden all that. Especially Rowan's wedding dress. Christ, Gordie, I was *there*, in the house when you found it."

"I'm sorry. I wasn't ready to tell anyone and Steve has given me enough grief over it for everyone so you don't have to worry about my lack of disclosure going unpunished," she said with a cheeky little smile.

Kat held up a hand again. "Do not tell me about Steve's punishments."

Gordie's grin said it all. It thrilled Kat to see her so in love.

"I'm glad you're happy." She pulled her sister into a tight hug. "You deserve so much and I'm so glad you finally let Steve in. He'd give you the moon if you let him."

"I know." Gordie gave her a squeeze. "You deserve every-thing too. Don't do what I did. Don't let something pass you by because it's not in the *plan*."

"I'm not—"

"Don't lie to me. Lie to yourself if you have to, but you can't lie to me." Gordie let go and gripped Kat's shoulders, holding her at arm's length. "I know what it looks like, Kat. I stared at that lie in the mirror every day for years. It cost me years of happiness, almost cost me my life and it definitely came close to costing me the best future I could wish for because I refused to let Steve in. Don't be me. Let Brady in."

"It's not like that."

"Oh, really?" Gordie asked with a skeptical arch of her eyebrow and tilt of her head.

"Okay, fine." Kat pulled away and paced behind her desk, swung around, and took the three steps back again. "He's my mate."

"What?" Gordie's eyes popped wide, her mouth dropped open, then closed, opened, closed. "Mate," she whispered. "Are you sure?"

"Sure as I can be." She shrugged. "He has my coyote clawing to get out so she can roll over and offer her belly. She's never done that for a man before."

"Wow. Okay. Okay. So you really do need to apologize then."

Kat had to agree with her sister. Even if she hadn't decided to accept the mating bond with Brady, she needed to make peace with him. Needed to get to know him again. For her sake as well as his, she needed to forget his last name and all the trouble his family had caused hers.

6

BRADY HATED BEING idle so by the time he'd made sure the house was sturdy and not going to fall down around his ears, he'd started in on the renovations he'd planned out in his head.

It probably would have been better to get a builder's input but he'd worked on enough barns, sheds, and the occasional house over the years to know to check for structural support before tearing down a wall.

He'd been in the roof cavity and besides the boxes of junk and dust, he'd determined the wall between the two back bedrooms did nothing but divide the space. In his head he saw this whole rear area as a master suite.

Taking out the separating wall between the rooms would allow for a king bed and walk-in closet. He'd leave the bathroom as is for now but later he'd turn that space plus a section of the current master bedroom into an en suite and separate half-bath for guests.

That was a long way off though. He just couldn't stand doing nothing, and seeing how he had the skills, it made sense to get a start on what he wanted. It wasn't like he'd be putting anyone except himself out with the noise and mess.

He'd definitely have to engage a builder at some point in the future. He might be able to swing a hammer and throw up dry wall, but he wasn't dumb enough to tackle a second story addition without professional help, and he wanted to re-use the new roof if possible, which would definitely require an expert's opinion and know-how.

The rumble of an engine growing louder had Brady downing tools and gloves, brushing off the dust, and moving toward the front of the house. He wasn't expecting anyone although he wouldn't be averse to having a visitor. He'd always been content with his own company, but the last few days had worn on his nerves.

Then again, it could be the lingering sense of danger that seemed to permeate the house—hover in the air—that had him moving quietly around the place like he had as a kid, not staying still long enough to get in trouble.

Just this morning he'd dropped a mug in the kitchen, spilling hot coffee everywhere, and he'd flinched waiting for the slap to the back of his head his father would have delivered when Brady was younger.

Yeah, he might not be expecting anyone, but he could do with a little social interaction right now.

Stepping out on the porch, he squinted his eyes against the glare of sunlight off snow. The small windows in the back rooms didn't allow much light in. He'd have to think about replacing them with bigger ones or putting in one big one, instead of two, maybe some French doors that opened onto a small deck where he could add a hot tub.

Hmm...he really liked that idea. He'd have to pace it out later to be sure it wouldn't encroach on the yard too much.

He raised a hand to shield his eyes and focused on the direction the engine roar came from. It wasn't the driveway, whatever machine headed toward him—definitely a vehicle of some kind—came from the forest beyond the old crumbling half garage attached to the left of the house.

Brady frowned.

That had to come down. He'd build a full garage before next winter.

As he was contemplating the size of add-on needed, a large dark blur whipped around the outer edge of the lopsided building, spraying snow as it turned, and he blinked.

Was that a snowmobile towing a...

Rubbing a fist over each eye, he concentrated on the sight in front of him.

Yep. A snowmobile pulling a sled. He couldn't tell by looking who was driving but his coyote instincts certainly knew.

Ren.

Brady didn't know what to think. It had been five days since the scene in her cafe.

Five days of wondering if she'd ever come around. Wondering what he could do to help change her mind about him.

Seeing Gordie—now known as Doc—at the clinic when he'd followed Doc Monroe that first day had given him hope that he could regain Ren's favor. Neither Monroe had said a word against him. Or his brother, for that matter, and if anyone had the right to hold animosity, it was Gordana Monroe.

The only time any of his family were mentioned was when

they'd asked him what he wanted to do with the bodies of his brother and father. He hadn't known they had kept his father on ice since last year. Gordie had explained their reluctance to bury him but also confessed to wanting to use his body for research.

Brady had no opinion on that. He actually didn't care what they did with his father. They'd never been close. The role of favorite son had gone to Marcus, and look what that had gotten him. Brady was more than happy to have been the forgotten one.

He watched Ren maneuver the snowmobile to position the sled close to the house. He'd offer to help, but at this point he couldn't be sure she wasn't here to kill him and load his body on that sled to be carted off into the mountains and buried, never to be found.

Grinning at the thought, Brady watched his mate carefully. Hoping for any clue that would indicate her mood or reason for being here.

When the engine switched off, Ren removed her goggles and gloves, and remained sitting on the big machine while she gave him a once over.

"So you are alive then," she called out with a smirk.

"Was there doubt?" He walked down the steps to join her in the yard. A yard he'd spent two days clearing of as much snow as he could.

"Some." She glanced at the house behind him. "No one seemed to know what condition this place was in or whether you came with supplies, and you haven't been to town since you arrived."

He couldn't hold back a grin. "Checking up on me?"

"Hell no! Damn old codgers won't shut up about you. I can't serve a drink or meal without one of them telling me something about the *prodigal son.*"

Brady frowned. "Prodigal doesn't seem the right word..."

"No, but those old coots think it is. I'm not going to point out their mistake. Besides, it would just keep them talking about you."

"Oh, and you can't have that." To avoid digging deeper into their—her—animosity, he tipped his chin toward the sled and asked, "What's all that?"

Ren hopped off the snowmobile and headed for her cargo. "I brought you a few things."

He was so shocked by her words that she had the straps off and the cover thrown back to reveal bags and boxes of supplies before he could get his brain to work and engage his mouth. At a complete loss for words, Brady stood there open-mouthed while Ren picked up a box and turned.

"Y-you brought me food?" he finally stammered, disbelief clear in his voice and no doubt on his face.

She shrugged, the box lifting in her arms. "Just a few things."

Grinning he stepped closer. "You were worried about me."

"No. There's a storm rolling in late tonight, early tomorrow. We're expecting a few days of solid snowfall, about two feet worth, and I don't want my sister to have to come out here to recover your body when you freeze or starve to death."

He moved closer, pressed his torso right up against her forearms, trapping them between his chest and the box. "You *were* worried about me," he whispered, the hope bursting to life inside him dripping from each word.

"No." She tilted her chin up a notch. "I'd be worried about anyone stuck out in the middle of nowhere."

"Really? So you've been dropping off supplies all over the mountain this morning?" Brady knew she hadn't. The flush in her cheeks wasn't only due to the cold. They'd gotten rosier the more he talked, the closer he'd gotten.

"No. Jeez. Here." She shoved into him making him take a step back and grab the box. "Just take that inside already."

A smile on his face, Brady did as directed. He wouldn't tell her he'd planned to make a trip into town this afternoon. He'd arrived with enough food and water to get him through two weeks but that had been more a precaution than necessity, and the trip to town was more about seeing Ren than picking up supplies.

He thought the house would be without running water or electricity when he arrived so he'd come prepared. It had been a pleasant surprise to find both still functioning once he'd fired up the generator that wasn't as old as he'd assumed it would be.

The supply of fuel he found in the garage would last at least a month and the fairly new furnace in the basement proved more than adequate to heat the three bedroom house once he'd fiddled with the thermostat.

"It's not as bad as I thought it would be," Ren observed behind him.

Glancing over his shoulder, he saw she had a second over-loaded box in her arms. He ignored her comment and asked, "How much stuff did you bring me?"

Her cheeks blushed a deeper pink and she looked away before saying, "Just some staples."

Brady looked in the box he put on the kitchen table, then the one she placed beside it. "And by staples you mean the whole grocery store?" he asked with a raised brow.

It didn't look as though she'd forgotten anything; there was even a two-pack of toilet paper. Without a word, she spun on her heel and headed back out front.

Sighing, he followed. "Ren."

"It's Kat," she argued. "No one calls me Ren anymore."

The tone of her voice told him the subject of why was off limits. He'd get to the bottom of that though. After talking with

Doc Monroe and Gordie—he couldn't get used to thinking of Gordie as Doc yet—the other day, he had a horrible suspicion that the name change was about him.

He couldn't imagine what it had been like for her when he'd disappeared. They'd been inseparable and he'd left without a word. Obviously he'd hurt her. If she'd felt anywhere near the level of pain he had over losing her, he could understand why she'd be so angry at him.

Why she'd not want anything to do with anyone named Connelly. In one way or another they'd all hurt her deeply.

Brady had a lot of making up to do. And he'd need to explain why he'd left, why he hadn't contacted her. He just hoped she could forgive him. For now he'd do everything he could to show her he was nothing like his brother or father and that he and his mother had been as much victims of their violence as the Whispering Mountain pack.

"Okay, Kathren, let me get that," he said, moving around her to pick up the box she reached for.

"Sure." She stepped back, her arms folded over her chest, eyes narrowed.

He scanned the sled as he grabbed the box and stopped. "Is all this for me?" Jesus. She really hadn't left anything out if this was all meant for him.

"Yes."

Brady could tell she didn't want to admit that, but what else could she do? She was here, with all these supplies; there was no denying she'd gotten them for him. Struck by a sudden thought, he asked, "How much do I owe you?"

"Nothing."

"Ren—" He froze at the look on her face.

"Nothing," she said with a stubborn tip of her chin.

"I can't let you—"

"You owe me nothing."

There was something playing in her eyes, something he thought he should know, except she pushed past him to grab more supplies before he could figure it out.

Leaving it for now, he headed into the house to unload. By the time they'd brought everything inside, he'd worked out his next step.

"Let me fix us some lunch. It's the least I can do after all this."

"Can you cook?" Ren inquired, one dark eyebrow arching.

He grinned. "I can open a tin of soup. Slap some cheese on bread."

"Ha." She unzipped her jacket, slipped it off her shoulders, and dropped it over the back of a chair before rummaging through a bag. "Good thing I brought a few ready meals then. I don't have time to whip something up."

Ready meals? Brady's smile spread as he set about emptying the bags and boxes and putting the food away while Ren organized lunch.

She might be saying one thing but she definitely meant another. The woman had brought pre-made food. She'd been more than worried about him. She'd thought about him for a while if all the containers of food ready to go in the freezer were an indication.

Maybe, like him, she hadn't been able to think about anything other than their connection since they'd laid eyes on each other five days ago.

He wasn't stupid though. He'd keep his mouth shut for now. One step at a time.

She was here. At his house. And she wasn't yelling at him or throwing him out. Progress.

The one thing that really gave him hope was all the supplies she'd brought with her.

She was taking care of him. She might not want to call it that, but he saw it for what it was.

Ren looked after those she cared about.

Brady wasn't sure what had happened or changed since he'd seen her last but he wasn't going to look a gift horse in the mouth. He'd take it as a good sign and not question it further.

As far as he was concerned they were heading in the right direction and he hadn't had to do a thing.

With effort, he'd have her loving him again in no time.

7

KAT WAS grateful that Brady hadn't pressed her about what she'd done. She couldn't really explain her actions to herself so telling him was out of the question.

She'd spent the last five days on tenterhooks waiting for him to show up at the Den. It had never entered her mind that he would take her at her word. She thought for sure he'd be there the next day. Or even after he'd dealt with the details of his brother's body that first day.

Instead he'd gone away and not come back. She couldn't explain the pain that brought her. She hadn't been surprised though. He'd left before. She'd expected him to leave again.

Why she'd thought that, she didn't know. It wasn't as though he'd made a habit of leaving exactly; he'd only ever done it once. Except he'd disappeared without a word. And not one since either. Her subconscious obviously thought he'd repeat that behavior even if her mind had started to see what little choice he would have had in the decision to leave Whispering Springs.

When Brady and his mother had first disappeared, his

father had told everyone they'd gone to visit a sick relative and would be back. Days turned into weeks turned into months, and before she knew it, he'd been gone a year and no one seemed to acknowledge their absence. Least of all his brother and father.

Kat hadn't understood it as a teenager and in the years since, with an adult perspective, she still didn't understand.

She wanted to know why he'd gone. *Where* he'd gone. Why he never contacted her. Why he hadn't come home before now.

In the years since Brady disappeared, Kat thought she'd moved past the betrayal she'd felt when he left. The last few days—and lectures from her sister—had proven that a lie. In spite of the hurt he'd inflicted all those years ago, she still loved him.

She'd loved him with a young girl's heart, an innocent, naive love that hadn't died when Brady left. That young, fragile emotion had lain dormant, hidden in some recess of her heart only to be resurrected the minute he walked into her cafe.

Resurrected with the fiery blaze of a mates connection.

It explained a lot about her interactions with men, that was for sure.

She'd messed around with a few boys back in high school. Even dated a couple of men in the years since then, except none of them had inspired more than curiosity or a second date. There was no burn of desire. No urge to strip off clothes and get as close as possible like there was with Brady.

Jeez, more than once over the years, she'd entertained the idea she was frigid.

Brady had proven that notion wrong.

Her body had been in a state of simmering arousal since he'd arrived.

As she'd done for the last week, she ignored the demands of her body and coyote, and concentrated on getting lunch heated.

She'd decided on beef stew. It would warm them up, and she'd been told by many it was one of her best meals.

Not that she was out to impress Brady with her cooking. Nope. She had no interest in dazzling him with her culinary skills.

He moved behind her where she stood at the ancient stove stirring the stew. "What is that?" he asked over her shoulder.

The kitchen was small, the stove in one corner where if someone wanted to see what she was cooking, they'd have to get up close. Real close. She tried to ignore the heat from his body, the warmth of his breath washing over the side of her face where he leaned forward.

The cool scent of forest and man overtook the smell of beef and vegetables warming in the saucepan and Kat's coyote stretched, rumbled a growl of pleasure at her mate's scent. Swallowing thickly, she managed, "Beef stew."

"Smells amazing. Sure beats canned soup."

"Canned soup?" She spun around, the breath sucking from her lungs at just how close he stood. If she breathed deeply, her breasts would touch his chest. They were almost eye-level. He had a couple of inches on her, and this close she could see the flecks of gold in his brown eyes. Licking her lips, she lowered her gaze to his chin and murmured, "Please tell me you've been eating something better than canned soup since you got here."

"I won't lie to you ever again, Ren." He trailed a fingertip down her cheek, over her jaw and, pressing under her chin, he applied pressure until she looked up and met his gaze. "I couldn't help breaking my promise before but I don't plan to ever break one again. So, yes, I've been living on canned soup."

Canned soup? What was he talking about? The only thing she understood was the fire blazing beneath her skin. The growl of her coyote as she clambered to be free. Free to take her mate. Be taken by him.

"Ren?" His finger left her skin.

"Huh?"

"The stew's boiling over."

"What? Oh!" Spinning around she switched off the heat and searched for steady ground. What the hell was that? He'd barely touched her and completely short circuited her brain.

She knew part of it was they were mates. The mating bond was sharp and fierce and hard to deny. Except she had to.

He needed to explain. She needed to understand.

No mating bond was going to dictate what happened in her life. If she was going to be with Brady—and right now she couldn't deny that was a probability—they needed to clear the air.

Jumping his bones, while appealing, wasn't why she'd come here today.

Kat needed to remember nothing and no one forced her hand. If she didn't want to mate Brady, she didn't have to. It was a shame she could no longer say with one hundred percent certainty she believed that.

Clearing her throat she asked, "Got clean plates?" while checking she hadn't burned the stew.

"Sure." Brady stepped away, taking his heat with him, leaving a chilled shiver racing over her skin in his absence.

Drawing in a deep breath, Kat tried to clear her mind of anything except putting food in front of them. She'd never had to deal with a raging libido before and wasn't sure she had the strength to deny their attraction.

That scared her.

The knowledge that Brady could distract her from anything and everything didn't sit well. For a woman used to being in control, having a man—a mate—snatch it away so easily was a terrifying prospect.

She might not know this grown-up Brady, but she'd loved

the young Brady with her whole heart. If she couldn't trust him to be careful with her heart—and her heart would definitely be involved—they could hurt each other badly.

She cursed her lack of relationship skills. She'd never had a boyfriend, never let anyone as close as Brady had once been. Kat wasn't stupid enough to deny Brady's leaving was the reason for that. He'd cut her open, left her behind, and as far as she knew, he hadn't looked back. Except maybe he had. She wouldn't know until she asked him.

Biting her tongue, she filled the bowls Brady put on the counter beside her and held in all her questions.

There would be time to ask; she wasn't rushing into anything, not with the way her mind and heart and coyote were at war over what to do.

Her coyote wanted to lie down, roll over, and offer him her belly—her throat.

Her heart yearned for the love they'd once shared with the deeper adult connection their age hadn't allowed before.

Her head, well her head was screaming at her to run. Run far away because it knew once she let Brady in, she'd let him in completely, and this time, if he left she'd be slashed to ribbons and never recover.

Except had she? Had she ever recovered from the first time?

The roiling emotions she'd experienced when she'd seen him in the Den said she hadn't gotten over his betrayal at all. She needed closure on that part of their lives. Needed to understand why he'd left and why he'd never come back or contacted her in all these years.

"Ask me."

Kat's gaze snapped up to meet Brady's. "What?"

"I can all but hear your brain spinning with questions. Ask me, Ren."

"Okay." She put her spoon down, her stomach rolling at the thought of getting answers. "Why did you leave?"

"Because my mother told me to."

"Well, yeah, I guessed that, but why did she leave? Why did she take you away from here and never come back?"

"Do you remember the year Brogan and Rowen's parents died?"

"Yes. Their car slid off the road and they crashed into a tree. Dad said both of them died on impact."

"That was the night Mom packed up a few of our belongings and drove us off the mountain."

"Why? I don't understand. She left Marcus behind, and your father."

"Let me tell you what happened and then you can ask any other questions."

Kat nodded.

"Dad came home, smashed through the front door naked and yelling. At first I thought he was drunk. It wouldn't have been the first time he'd loaded up and gone off except that night was different. I didn't understand why until he mentioned the Wilders were dead. Yelled now that he was sovereign he could clear the pack of non-bloods and half-bloods, return the pack to being pure instead of tainted by human blood."

She opened her mouth but closed it when Brady shook his head.

"Mom ask him why he thought the Wilders were dead, and he looked at her like she was stupid. He backhanded her, sending her to the floor as he yelled he'd killed them. Shouted no self-respecting full-blood coyote should saddle himself with a human wife and half-blood children never mind be allowed to lead a pack with them by his side."

"But they crashed, went off the side of the road."

"I don't know the details of the crash, but if I know

anything about my father I know he would have had supporters get rid of any evidence that pointed to the accident being anything except an accident."

"Oh." She could see Malcolm Connelly doing that. And she remembered when he first took over as sovereign he had a lot of supporters on the council and in the sheriff's department. That had changed during his reign of terror but before that, yeah, she could definitely see him getting someone to clean up after him.

"The look on your face tells me he could have covered it up."

Nodding, Kat said, "Yes, back then he had people on his side who would have helped."

"After more yelling, a few more smacks for Mom, a punch for me, and a smile for Marcus, he left. Everything moved quickly after that. Mom packed a couple of bags, left everything else, and told us to get in the truck. Marcus refused, called her all sorts of names, and said he was going to tell Dad we'd left. I think it was the last part that made Mom realize we had to go or we weren't going.

"She climbed into the driver's seat and drove. Hours and hours she drove and cried, and I couldn't do anything. Not then, not before, not after. We drove straight through to Nebraska and arrived at the house of a friend she'd known before she met Dad. A man she'd gone to school with; at one point they'd been a couple and I don't know how or why they separated and she ended up with Dad, but Mom and Hank were soul mates."

"Nebraska? How did she end up here?"

Brady shrugged. "I don't know. I wish I did. I still don't really understand why she wanted us to leave. I get Dad was abusive, but from what I remember, he'd always been that way, and that night wasn't any worse than all the others so why did she want to leave? Why did she forbid me from contacting anyone here?"

"Sounds like you have just as many questions as I do."

"I do. And I might have a way of finding some answers but I need help."

Kat didn't know how he could find answers when all the key players were dead, but if there was a way she'd help. "How? Help with what?"

"Mom left boxes. I haven't gone through them but I know there are journals in there. From the first day we arrived at Hank's she kept a journal. I have them all."

"Personal diaries? I'm not sure how I feel about reading someone's, your mother's, private thoughts."

"I'm not comfortable with it either except I think they hold the truth about that night and a lot more. I know we haven't seen each other in thirteen years, but if anyone besides me is going to read those journals, I want it to be you."

8

"HOW MANY MORE BOXES?" Ren asked as he added two more to the pile against the wall in the living room.

"A couple. Why?"

"These aren't just filled with journals," she explained while rummaging through one. "There are keepsakes from when you and Marcus were little, personal papers, pictures, school reports, other stuff."

"Okay, so we need to go through everything before we start reading the journals then." He turned to head back out for the last load.

"Wait. You want me to help with that? Don't you want to decide what to keep and what to throw out?"

There were a dozen boxes of various sizes lined up against the wall. On his own it would take him days, but with Ren's help they could gather things into piles by priority and work their way through in one or less. "Let me grab the last two boxes, then we'll start piles and decide what we should look at first."

"It would be quicker to decide what to keep and not while

we sort. If we sort then go through each pile, that's dealing with everything twice. Double handling is not an efficient way to do any job."

"Okay. We decide as we go. We'll need a throw, a keep, and a journal pile. We should keep those separate, right?"

Ren waved a hand toward the door. "Go get the rest, I'll grab a garbage bag for the stuff you want to get rid of, and once we empty a couple of boxes, we can store anything you want to keep in categories in separate boxes instead of having it all tossed in together like it is now. You might want to frame some of these pictures for the walls too so we should keep those separate from the other keepsakes your mother has in here."

Brady glanced around the room. The only thing filling the place was a worn couch and one chair; both items had been here when he was a kid. Everything else was stripped bare. Bare walls, bare mantle over the fireplace, bare shelves on the empty bookcase beneath the window.

He didn't recall his mother ever putting pictures up here. She'd filled Hank's house with them but here, in the mountain home she'd run from, she'd never displayed any. There had to be a reason for that.

Everything he'd learned in recent months pointed out he didn't know his mother as well as he thought he had. She had secrets. Secrets she'd taken to the grave if she hadn't written them down in one of the many journals scattered throughout these boxes.

It was a daunting task, going though all her things. He'd gotten rid of her clothes—and Hank's—before selling the farm, and Hank's estate paperwork had been dealt with by his lawyer. Hank hadn't had any family, which explained why he'd left the farm to Brady and his mom, so the decision on what to do with Hank's personal papers had fallen to them.

He'd kept the man's birth and death certificates as well as

the original deed to the farm. Anything that dealt with the business of the farm went to the new owners. It had taken months to go through everything after Hank's death. Brady hoped these boxes didn't take him as long.

His mother had been of no use without Hank, and Brady hadn't really known what to do with most things so had relied on advice from Hank's lawyer. Luckily the lawyer had also been a friend and he'd been more than happy to lend a hand outside of his legal obligation, but that was more confirming Brady's decisions than helping him make them.

Now Brady had Ren. He might not have her the way he wanted to, but he had her. By his side to walk down this path that left him feeling gutted before they'd even started.

"Thank you." He leaned over and brushed his lips on top of her head. "I don't think I'd have the nerve to do this yet if you weren't helping."

"Why? It's just boxes of papers and photos from your mother's life."

"Actually, I think what we've got here is the family closet."

"Meaning?"

"There are skeletons in here I'm not sure I want to dig up."

"If you want answers, we're going to find them buried with those bones."

Brady sighed. "I know. I just can't help wondering if it would be better to not know. I have a bad feeling what we find here is going to be far worse than anything we already know about."

"It might be." Ren pushed to her feet and stepped into him, wrapping her arms around his waist as she rested her cheek on his shoulder. "But, Brady, you're not the only one affected by what we find. We need to know if your father really did have something to do with the Wilders' deaths and why your mother thought she had to leave the mountain in the middle of the night without a word to anyone before or after."

"And why Marcus stayed." Slipping his arms around her, he pulled her closer, lowered his head to rest his cheek on her hair. "I'll never forgive him for breaking her heart."

"I'm not sure we'll ever find the answer to why he stayed other than Marcus idolized your father. I saw it after you were gone. He was also terrified of him. Everyone was. And when Malcolm showed up after we all thought he was dead, Rowen said he looked unhinged to her. As though he'd lost touch with reality. From what Gordie discovered he'd been doing, I have to agree with Rowen; his actions definitely say he'd gone insane."

"Marcus?"

"No. Malcolm. But then with everything Marcus did in recent months, he appeared to have gone crazy too."

"We need to talk to the sheriff. I'm supposed to talk to him about Marcus anyway, so I guess we'll ask about the Wilders' accident and my dad at the same time."

Ren pulled back and looked up at him. They were close in height but she still needed to tilt her head back a little to make eye contact. "You want me to go with you to see Dale?"

"Yes, of course, you volunteered to help, remember?"

"I volunteered to help read journals which somehow turned into sorting through boxes of personal effects and now talking to the sheriff. I've got a life you know. I can't just drop everything to be at your beck and call, Brady."

"I'm not asking you to do that. It won't be for a few days. We'll have to wait until this storm front moves on. In the meantime we'll go through my mom's things and see what we can find."

"I need to leave soon, and if we get the snow they're predicting, I won't be able to come back for a few days."

"Stay."

"What?" She jerked in his arms, tried to pull free, but he held on.

"If we get snowed in, you won't be opening the Den, right, because no one will be out and about. Stay here, help me use the time we'll be trapped indoors to go through everything."

"I—"

"*Please.*" He'd beg if he had too. He wanted her close. Wanted to be able to convince her they could be more than childhood friends. He couldn't do that if she went home.

She searched his eyes, looking for something he wasn't sure he understood but desperately wanted to give her. "I'll need to make a phone call and check on things before I can say yes." She stayed in his arms, studying him.

"Make the call."

Neither of them moved; lost in their own thoughts, they remained still, wrapped in each other's arms.

Brady took the time to catalogue the changes in her face from when they were kids. She was still the same Ren; the girl he'd loved had grown into a beautiful woman, there was no denying that, except there were subtle changes. Small lines beside her eyes, her hair was shorter than she used to keep it, and her body had developed curves in interesting places.

Places his body was all too aware of.

All those changes had barely begun when he'd left and he had to wonder if he was the only man who noticed her. Now or in the years he'd been gone.

"You don't have a boyfriend, do you?" he blurted before the thought even registered in his head.

"What?" She pulled away from him; breaking out of his hold, she took a step back and slammed her hands on her hips. "What kind of question is that? Do you think I'd be here with you, in your arms, if I did?"

"You're not here *with me* though, are you? And that was just a comforting hug between old friends, right?"

Her mouth opened. Closed. The ends tipped down.

"Forget I asked. It's none of my business."

"None of your business." Palms flat on his chest, she gave him a shove. "Of course it's your business, Brady Connelly, you're my *mate.*"

He sucked in a breath, every muscle snapping taut, his coyote howling with pleasure. Neither of them had voiced the mate thing out loud yet. Hearing her say it, admit it, had Brady's insides scrambling.

He wanted to throw her over his shoulder, find the nearest bed, and claim her.

Wanted to pick her up and spin her around.

Wanted to race outside and yell it for the mountain to hear.

"What are we going to do about that?" he asked instead.

"Nothing. Yet." She paced away from him. "I'm not ready for that. I don't think you are either. There's too much"—she waved a hand at the boxes—"to deal with before we deal with us."

"Is there an us?" Brady mentally crossed his fingers.

"I might not be ready for there to be, but I'm not stupid and I refuse to live in denial. We're mates and even if I'm not happy about it, that's our reality. And I'm okay with it, as long as you don't pressure me to accept you. I get that neither of us really has a choice in this, but I'll be damned if we're forced to do anything before we get our heads around it and I'd like to get to know you again before jumping into a mating bond. So, yes, there is an us, but we'll deal with it in a way that suits *us.*"

"Okay."

"Okay? Okay what? You're happy to wait until I'm ready?"

"Yes."

"Why do I not believe that?"

Brady laughed. "I'm not going to force you into anything, and I definitely won't be forcing myself on you. I will be honest about what I feel and the struggle I'm having waiting though. But you are right, there's far too much I need to deal with first. I want to put all of it behind us, put it in the past where it belongs, so when we are ready we'll be going forward with a clean slate."

"So we agree to put the mate thing aside and deal with all of this as friends."

"We're more than friends, Ren."

"Obviously. Still, we ignore all that for now."

"We can try. I don't know how successful we'll be. A mate connection is hard to ignore. It's the strongest connection there is, and we had it long before we knew what it was."

She tilted her head to the side, one eyebrow arching in question.

"You have to admit we were inseparable as kids. Our subconsciouses knew long before we did that we were meant to be together."

"I think our being mates explains a lot of things," she muttered.

"What?"

"Nothing." She gave his shoulder a push. "Go get the other boxes and I'll make that call."

"You didn't really answer my question."

"What question?"

"Do you have a boyfriend, Ren?"

She growled, her scowl cute in its fierceness. "*No.*"

"Good."

Before she could comment on his remark, he left the house and went to retrieve the last two boxes from the back of his truck. He hadn't bothered to bring them inside until now because he didn't want to deal with any of this. Except what he said to Ren was true. He—they—needed to put the past in the past and more forward with a clean slate. They deserved that.

And Whispering Springs deserved to know what his father had done.

Brady could only hope whatever his father had done hadn't left permanent scars.

Unfortunately, he thought those hopes would go unrealized. He had no idea what his father had been like outside of the house because Brady rarely spent time with him at home, never mind in town. Marcus truly had been the favored son and as bad as it was to think, he couldn't help but be grateful his brother had taken their father's affections.

Marcus had ended up dead, and Brady had to assume their father's influence had a lot to do with the outcome of his brother's life.

He'd struggled to understand how his mother could leave with only one son but maybe she knew something he didn't. Maybe there was something in her journals or papers that would explain everything.

"Hey, you bringing those boxes in? It's starting to snow."

Ren's words pulled him from his thoughts. He had no idea how long he'd stood there in a daze but she was right. The snow was coming down and it wasn't a light fall either. Glancing up, he scanned the sky. "The storm moved in early."

"Looks like it. Wendy said the sheriff was in to let all the out-of-towners know they should head on home before it got to the point they couldn't."

"Wendy?"

"My manager. She's keeping the Den open in case anyone gets stuck in town. She lives in one of the apartments above so she won't have to go out in the storm to get home."

"You're staying?"

Frowning, she turned her face up to look at the sky. "Yeah. Even if I hadn't decided to, I don't think I've got a choice now."

Brady turned to hide his smile. She might not be exactly happy to be staying with him but he'd work with what he could get. A lot had changed in just a few hours. With a day or two of snowed-in time he would have hours to convince her not only that their mating wasn't a bad thing, but it was something good.

9

BRADY PLACED the last journal on the second stack and leaned back against the couch. "That's it. That's all of them?"

"I've got half a box to finish yet, but there aren't any more journals in here." Ren continued to pull things from the box in front of her.

It was dark out; then again, it had gone dark hours ago when the storm closed in on them. He'd started a fire and the furnace was pumping warm air through all the rooms to ward off the cold. The wind still managed to sneak in. Through cracks in the walls and floors. Brady had been mentally adding things to his list of improvements throughout the afternoon.

"We should take a break when you finish and have some dinner."

"I put lasagna in the oven when I went to the bathroom. It should be ready soon," Ren admitted without looking up, her gaze intent on the paper she'd just pulled from the box.

"You already put dinner on?" She blew his mind. He hadn't thought about dinner until he'd gotten through all his boxes and checked his watch to see they'd been at it for hours. It had been even longer since they'd eaten anything.

"Hmm..." She was focused on the paper in her hand, her brow scrunching up, her lips moving as she silently read. "Brady, do you have another brother? Other than Marcus?"

"What? No, it was just me and Marcus." He straightened away from the couch. "Why?"

"This is a birth certificate for Jacob Connelly and if my math is right, he'd be about twenty-two."

"Four years *younger* than me?"

"Yeah. This is weird though. The mother is listed as Michelle Watson but the father is unknown. How can that be?"

What the fuck? His mother had another child? He couldn't remember her being pregnant or having a baby or there being any kids besides him and Marcus. And why would it list her maiden name? "I don't understand..."

"I'll put it with the journals. But it reminds me, did you find your birth certificate, or Marcus's?"

"No. They weren't in the boxes I went through. You didn't find them?"

Shaking her head, Ren kept studying the paper in her hand. "This is bizarre. I wonder if Dad would know about it? He would have taken care of your mom while she was pregnant. Probably attended the birth. He should have records of you and Marcus too."

"Does he keep records for that far back?"

"I think so. And I know Gordie scanned everything into a database when she took over the clinic so she'd have the information if it was recorded. Plus she's doing some kind of pack history thing where she's logging all members born in the pack, their family line, and where they are now."

"And if this Jacob wasn't recorded?" he asked, his gaze glued to the pile of journals. They looked innocent enough except they might hold an untold number of bombs within their pages.

"Then we hope the answers are in those books. Or maybe one of the older pack members would know. Possibly Grammy Brant."

"I'd have been four. You three. Gordie's the same age as Marcus, right? So they would have been nine? She might remember something. My mom being pregnant or a new baby."

"Maybe. But I don't remember all that much before I was around twelve."

"I guess I'm the same, but a baby is a significant event. And Gordie always struck me as super observant. She'd remember something like that. Especially seeing how all she ever wanted to do when we were little was play doctor."

"True. I'll send her a message after dinner."

Brady grabbed his phone. "We could call her now."

"It's not urgent. We'll have dinner and then I'll call. I know she doesn't hold a grudge against you but I'd like to handle this, if it's all right with you."

"You don't want me to talk to her? You think I'll upset her?"

"No. I know she doesn't blame you for what your brother and father did, and I'm glad for that. I just feel as though I should ask her this."

"Okay, but you know I have to talk to her about the bodies, right? It's not like I can avoid her forever. Not when we're..." He didn't say mates; he didn't have to. Ren might be ignoring it for now, but much like his mother's journals, their mate status affected more than them. Her family would have to accept their mating, and as far as he was concerned, the sooner the better. Of course he should probably wait until Ren accepted it. And agreed to the mating bond.

Sighing, she dropped the birth certificate next to the pile of journals. "You're right. I'm being stupid. Gordie might have moved on from the attack but it appears as if I'm still struggling with it."

"Wait. You were there? Did he hurt you?"

"What? Oh, no. I wasn't there until after. It might be easier to deal with if I had been there for the whole thing though. I'll never get over seeing Gordie lying in a pool of blood." She shuddered. "Even with the knowledge that it wasn't hers, I find it difficult to wipe that fear from my mind and heart."

"I'm sorry." If he'd packed up and moved back here right after his mother died instead of waiting months, he might have been able to get through to Marcus. Stop him from trying to kill Gordie.

"For what?"

"Marcus. If I'd been here maybe I could have—"

"No way." She sat up straight. "There is no way you could have done anything. God, we all knew he had been terrorizing Gordie and we still let her and a heavily pregnant woman go off alone. I'm just glad it turned out the way it did. Neither Gordie nor Tatum were badly hurt and they both seem to be doing well. Tatum and Dale have reconciled since then, so that was a good thing to come out of the attack."

"I just wish I'd been here."

"Why, so Marcus could have had another target? Don't for one minute think he would have welcomed you back with open arms. He'd isolated himself after your father died, well when we all thought he had, but I guess Marcus probably knew he wasn't dead the whole time. Then when Malcolm tried to run Quinn down and ended up really dead, your brother became even less sociable. Not that he ever was. From the time Malcolm became sovereign, Marcus acted as though everyone was beneath him and held himself apart from the rest of us."

"Dad's hatred of half-bloods and non-bloods would have influenced Marcus."

"Yes, they would have, and as much as I want to blame Marcus for that, I can't. Your father raised him, molded him." Ren shuffled on her knees until she knelt beside him. "And as much as I hated that you left, it probably saved you from a similar fate. I have to think your mother knew what would happen and tried to remove you both from Malcolm's orbit."

"I was never in his orbit. Marcus was always the favorite. Dad barely said two words to me most days. The only time he paid me any attention was when he needed someone to blame for something. And his fists did a lot of the talking then anyway."

"As much as I missed you, I'm thankful to your mother for taking you away from that. From him."

"I'm not sure I can be as generous. She cut away everything I'd ever known because of one man. I get that she felt it was her only option, and maybe it was, except she forbade me from contacting anyone here. She kept me from you and I can't forgive her for that."

"You will."

"I don't see how."

"She loved you enough to risk her life, Brady. If he'd caught you leaving..." A shudder wracked her. "She hurt you emotionally, and I have to believe she knew she would by insisting you not contact anyone. I know we don't know exactly what went on but I remember your mom, and what I remember is a woman who wasn't scared of facing Malcolm. I'd seen him get angry at her numerous times at the clinic when we were little. Something had to have happened for her to believe her only choice was to run and not look back."

"If what my father said about the Wilders is true, then I guess she thought he'd kill her if she stood in his way. I remember him yelling at her to keep her trap shut, something about not telling tales because accidents happened all the time."

Ren gasped, her hand reaching for his, gripping and squeezing tight. "He said something like that to me. It was after you were gone, after Gordie and Anthony had their accident."

"Anthony? What accident?"

"They were driving to the city for school when they were involved in a hit and run. Anthony died instantly and Gordie lost their baby while she was trapped in the wreck."

"When did this happen? After I left?"

"Yes, it was after that your dad made it clear I wasn't to mention you again."

"How? Why? You'll have to give it all to me, Ren. Why would he tell you not to mention me?"

"I asked Marcus about you but he wouldn't answer me, didn't say a word, and you know me, I don't give up so easily so I kept badgering him. Your father came up behind me, grabbed my arm, and told me not to mention you again. Then he warned me to be careful, that a half-blood like me didn't want to have an accident like my sister."

"Fucking hell." He reached over and pulled her against him. "I'm sorry he did that. Sorry I wasn't here to stop him."

Ren snuggled into his side, one hand pressed to his chest, her head resting on his shoulder. "You couldn't have stopped him. He was sovereign and he didn't directly threaten me."

"I wish he were alive so I could kill him," he growled. "I hope he died a painful death. He hurt so many people, tried to destroy so much... God. I can't believe I come from that."

"You're nothing like him."

"How do you know? You haven't seen me in a decade."

"I know you, Brady. I've always known you. Deep down where it matters."

She was right. And he could say the same about her. They

might not know the little things like favorite color or food but they knew each other's heart. It was too soon to declare his love but it was there—had always been there—warming his chest and now giving him hope for a future with her.

It explained his lack of interest in any other woman. He'd always been in love with Ren. Had been waiting for the day he could come back to her.

Would she think him an idiot for waiting? For hoping she'd be his first?

Would she think less of him because of his inexperience?

He should tell her before they went any further. She might not want to be with him once she knew the truth.

Brady stared down at the top of Ren's head. How did he tell her...he swallowed, took a deep breath, and jumped right in. "I've never had sex with a woman."

Her head tipped back, her long lashes fluttering, her brows pulling in, a delicate wrinkle forming between them. "You're gay?" she asked in a whisper filled with disappointment and disbelief.

"No! Jesus, fuck no." He shook his head. "Why would you even think that?" Grabbing her hand, he placed it over his hard cock. "Have you not seen the way I react to you? Fuck, it doesn't matter how many times I jerk off, I can't get the damn thing to go down."

"But you just said..." Her eyes slowly widened, her fingers twitching on his denim covered shaft, as the true meaning of his words registered. "Holy shit. You've never had sex?"

For a second she remained wide-eyed, incredulity written all over her face, and Brady felt his own face heat with embarrassment. Then her expression cracked, she pulled away, doubled over, and laughed her ass off.

For a stunned moment he remained silent, then emotion flooded him. "What the hell is funny about this?"

"Sorry," she gurgled, her laughter scrambling her words. "Give me. A sec."

Brady crossed his arms and waited for Ren to get herself under control. The embarrassment of moments ago was quickly overshadowed by anger. There wasn't anything funny about being a twenty-six year old virgin.

It hadn't been a conscious decision. His mother had been quite adamant that he not jump into sex when he was a teenager. She made it perfectly clear what the consequences of such an act could be and he'd heeded her warnings.

And if he were honest, he hadn't met anyone who made him want to change his decision because he wasn't looking. He knew who he wanted. Ren. He wanted the girl he'd been in love with all his life.

The one who was busting a gut laughing at him.

10

KAT PULLED in a breath and tried to stop laughing.

Jesus. They were fucked.

Or not.

That thought had her snorting a giggle.

Shit. This was not going the way she thought it would. Neither of them had any practical experience and they were fighting a mating bond that amplified hormones.

Humans thought teenagers were horny; they had nothing on a coyote shifter in the middle of a mating dance.

"Damn. We're in trouble," she mumbled.

Brady frowned. "Well, someone is."

Kat stared at him as she pulled in deeper breaths and found some level of normalcy. He sat there with his arms crossed, face in a menacing scowl, and in spite of the anger rolling off him, she couldn't ignore the embarrassment and disappointment swirling in his eyes, or the arousal buzzing in her veins.

She had to clear the air. Make him understand she wasn't laughing at him. She was laughing at the situation they found themselves in.

"We both are."

He cocked one eyebrow but the scowl remained.

"We're on the same page."

"Huh?"

"We're starting this at the same place."

Shaking his head, he dropped his arms to his sides, and hands clenched, growled, "Stop talking in riddles. Why the fuck are we both in trouble?"

"Because neither of us knows what we're doing here."

"Of course not, we haven't found our mates until now."

Seemed she wasn't the only one slow on the uptake today. She couldn't believe for one second she'd thought he was trying to tell her he was gay. She'd spent most of the day trying to ignore the bulge in his pants, the hungry looks, the sensual brush of fingers when they'd passed things back and forth.

"No. We haven't. But it's the fact that neither of us have had sex before that means we're in trouble."

His mouth dropped open, snapped shut. Nostrils flaring, he dragged in a deep breath. "We're both virgins?" he asked in a strangled voice.

Kat nodded.

It was slow, but Brady's lips curled up and parted to reveal straight white teeth. She'd say the smile looked wolfish but he was a coyote and that would be an insult. Whatever she called it, that curve of his mouth telegraphed loud and clear that he was pleased by her revelation.

"You're happy about that?"

"Hell, yes. It means no one else will ever touch you. You're mine. Only mine."

"Ah, okay, that sounds a little too alpha for me." A shiver of excitement traveled over her skin, making her words a lie. She definitely liked his alpha vibe.

"The reverse applies."

"The reverse?"

"You'll be the only one to ever touch me."

"Oh." A curl of pleasure unfurled in her belly. The thought of being the first to touch Brady, to give him pleasure, had her coyote rumbling in approval.

"We get to explore together."

"Explore?" God, she sounded like a parrot. She'd never had her mind confused by lust before. Would it always be like this?

"Sex. We get to explore sex together."

"Explore sex..." Okay. She could get behind that. Now that she actually *wanted* sex, she could think of numerous things she wanted to try. Except... Sighing, she said, "We can't."

"What? Why not?"

"Because I'm not ready to be marked—mated."

"We can still fool around some."

"No. We can't." Shaking her head, she explained, "I've heard the mating connection amplifies our sensitivity. It's how Brogan marked El before she even knew coyote shifters existed."

"El? Brogan's mate?"

"Yes, she's the woman Rowen lived with when she left the mountains."

"Rowen left Whispering Springs?"

"Oh shit." She shook her head. "I forget you haven't been here. You don't know everything that happened since..."

"I want to know. I want you to share everything with me."

"Some of it involves Marcus and your dad. And those parts aren't good."

Brady took a deep breath. "Doesn't matter. I want to know it all."

"Why don't we start with all the mates? Brogan is mated to El. She's Australian and has a really cool accent. Then there are Rowen and Quinn. Everyone knew that would happen since they were younger, so when she came home, nobody was surprised they mated straight away. They're the reason El came here even though she was human and we don't usually let them this high on the mountain. Gordie and Steve—"

"Steve McKenna?"

"Yes. They're true mates unlike her and Anthony."

"Anthony?"

"He was a distant cousin to the Brants. Came to live here a few years before you left. You don't remember him?"

Shaking his head, he said, "No, but he doesn't matter, Gordie's with Steve now."

"Yes, they got together at Christmas but they've been doing the dance for years. Gordie was being stubborn."

"Runs in the family."

"What does?"

"Nothing." He did a rolling motion with his hand. "Go on."

"Right, Dale and Tatum would be next. He came home over a year ago and Tatum followed just this past Christmas. There's a huge story there but I don't know all the details. Something about them having a third mate who died. I'm not sure what that means, but I do remember Cade from when we were younger. He and Dale were best friends and always together, remember?"

"I think I remember them. And they both mated Tatum? Tatum Brant?"

"Apparently."

"Interesting. I remember Dad saying something about William Brant's half-blood granddaughter once. Before his hatred of non-bloods extended to half-bloods, he tried to talk Marcus into dating her but she was a few years younger than him; I think she's younger than us too. Anyway, Marcus said he wasn't into fucking little girls."

"Jesus. He said that?"

"If I'm remembering right, she hadn't shifted for the first time yet. So Marcus might have been crude but he was right."

"I'm not sure how much longer your dad pushed the Tatum thing because at some point Marcus turned his sights on Rowen. His obsession led him to attack her one day and she, like you, disappeared in the middle of the night. She stayed away six years. Long enough for Brogan and Quinn to take over as sovereign and regal."

"A lot has happened in thirteen years."

"It has. Let's leave the rest of the history lesson for later." She pushed to her feet and offered her hand. "Dinner, then I'll call Gordie about taking a look at those records."

"Okay, I'll take care of the dishes while you call your sister."

It didn't take them long to get dinner on the small, scarred table in the pokey little dining room. Most of the furniture was worn, old, and Kat wondered if Brady would want to replace it with his own things.

Brady ignored his food and looked around the room. "What do you think about taking down the walls between here and the kitchen and living room?" He pointed to the walls behind her and opposite.

Kat swallowed the bite of lasagna she'd just taken. "Me?"

"Yes, you. What do you think? The kitchen is too small as is and you'll want a bigger oven for starters, a bigger refrigerator too, so we should plan the space to accommodate larger appliances as well as an island counter I think."

"Me?" she squeaked. "Why would you need my opinion or preferences?"

His gaze returned to hers. "Because this will be our home and I want you to have input. The place needs renovating, bringing up to date, and I want you to have the things you like and need."

"Brady. I can't move in with you. You've just come back. Besides, I have my apartment above the Den—"

"You're my mate. We're going to eventually complete the bonding and I want you to live here. I don't care if it's tomorrow, next week, next year—okay, fine, next year better not be on option," he said with a grin. "But this place needs love and care and I want us both to give it that love and care. I want to give it to you, too, want you to give it to me."

"I." Kat closed her mouth. Swallowed. She had no idea what to say.

"Honestly, no pressure. I get that we need to work our way up to that point but I've got two months before I start work at Wild Encounters and I want to do some of the renovations before then. I already started knocking down the wall between the two back bedrooms in prep for the new master suite."

"You knocked down a wall? Do you even know how to do that?"

"Sure." He grinned. "You just take to it with a sledge hammer."

"Brady!" Was he crazy? "You can't just knock down walls. You have to check the roof won't cave in, make sure there aren't any electrical wires or water pipes..." She took in his smile, the twinkle in his eyes. "You know all that, don't you?"

"I may have done construction and demolition work before. I checked all those things. But don't worry. I plan to consult a builder about the second story addition."

"Second story..."

"Yes. I thought we'd put a second story on so we didn't take up any more yard space. I figured four bedrooms for the kids and possibly a fifth for guests."

"Four?"

"You don't want four?"

"Brady, I haven't even thought about having one, never

mind four."

"We should probably talk about that. I'd like four. How many do you want?"

"I." She closed her eyes. He was doing her head in. She hadn't decided to accept their mating bond yet and he was planning their home and how many children they would have. "Brady, I can't," she sighed.

"Okay, forget about that. Tell me what your ideal kitchen would look like."

Opening her eyes, Kat stared at the man who'd been her childhood friend. He'd been her best friend. The one she told all her secrets too, the one who'd told her his. She remembered talking about what they wanted to do as adults. Brady had wanted to be a forest ranger so he could protect the mountains, and she'd wanted to run the Den.

She'd achieved her goal; had he?

"What will you be doing at Wild Encounters?"

"Taking treks into the mountain. Day treks and overnighters."

"Like a forest ranger?"

Brady laughed. "God, you remember that? Yeah, I guess in a way I'm like a forest ranger. Except I get to tell people what to do and what not to do on the treks. As a ranger, I wouldn't really have that much control over what people did, and I'd have to work within the constraints of a human government employer. At least working for Brogan and Quinn I can help other shifters as well as the forest and animals that call it home."

"You dreamed of being a ranger."

"I did. But this is better. And I get to be here in Whispering Springs. I finally got to come home."

Kat smiled. "I'm glad you're here."

He reached across the table and grabbed her hand. "In case

you're wondering, when I say home, I don't just mean this house or the mountain. I mean you, Ren."

"I don't want to rush."

"I know."

"But I do want to move forward." What she really wanted was to kiss him but she wasn't sure they could stop at one.

"Okay."

"And I think we can explore sex without marking each other."

"Oh, how?" His hand tightened around hers.

"We can relieve some of this tension, make the whole thing less stressful."

"How? I can't be in a room with you and not want inside you," he said. The muscles in his arm where it rested on the table quivered, in fact his whole body vibrated in his seat. He was holding back. Letting her lead when clearly he wanted to take control.

"Okay, I get that. I want that too. Eventually, but... I'm not ready to close the deal. It feels like I'm on a runaway train and there's nothing I can do to stop it except slow it down a bit. Give myself—*us*—some time to think about this."

"I don't need time." Brady dropped her hand and stood; stepping around the table he moved toward her. "I know what I want. What I've always wanted. It's why I waited."

"Fuck, Brady, don't lay that on me. No pressure, right?"

"Sorry. I'm trying. Honestly. But this need for you is riding me harder than any mountain trek I've been on. I'm sweating and out of breath and shaking, and goddammit, I think I'm going to lose my mind if I don't get inside you soon."

She could see he was struggling, maybe more than she was because she wanted to hold back. He didn't. He wanted to barrel into this thing full speed, arms wide open. Kat didn't know if she could do that.

On some level, she trusted him. Believed he wouldn't leave again and yet... "I can't do it. Not now."

Sucking in a breath, he ran a hand down his face. "Okay. Okay. Tell me what you're thinking."

"We make ourselves come. In front of each other."

"You want to watch me jerk one off?"

"Yes. But I'll be doing the same." She glanced toward the bedrooms. "I can lie on the bed while you sit in a chair across the room."

"Christ." He scrubbed a hand down his face again. "You're trying to kill me."

"No. I'm not. This is just as hard for me but I need to be in control of this. I can't—won't—dive right in. It doesn't matter how much my coyote wants that."

"It might be better if you're in one room and I'm in another. I'll know what you're doing and I'll smell you but I won't be able to see you."

She smiled. "We could try phone sex."

A shudder wracked him, and he shoved both hands through his hair and yanked. "Jesus. You really are trying to kill me."

She laughed. "Pretty sure the killing is mutual."

And it was. But in spite of the struggle it would be to watch Brady get off, she needed to see it. Needed her own relief too. Kat feared if they didn't do something to relieve the tension winding them both tighter with every second they were together, it would snap. She wasn't sure that was the way to go with this whole mate thing.

Actually, she wasn't sure mutual masturbation was the right thing either, except now she'd voiced the suggestion, she couldn't stop the reel of images flickering through her head.

If they did this, took the pressure off, maybe she'd get her wish. Maybe they could kiss without the threat of ripping each other's clothes off.

11

THEY WERE quiet as they finished dinner, Brady didn't know about Ren but all he could think about was getting to see her naked, getting to watch... Shuddering, he picked up his plate and stood.

"I'll get started on the dishes." He turned his back and left the room. Hopefully being separated by walls would help relieve some of the tension twisting his insides.

His reprieve was short lived when Ren entered the kitchen and moved in beside him at the sink a moment later.

"The call wouldn't connect. The storm must have knocked service out," she explained, picking up the dish towel and reaching for the cutlery he'd washed.

"Maybe try again," he offered.

"Later."

The anticipation of what they planned hung in the air, making Brady twitchy, his pulse pound, his breathing shallow. His body had been on hyper alert since he'd sensed Ren in the cafe days ago and now that she was here, now that he'd spent hours with her, the slightest thing threatened to set him off.

He'd been aroused before; every teenage boy went through nights of wet dreams and days of ill-timed boners—coyote shifters were no different. Only this felt like he'd mainlined a gallon of coffee laced with crack. His heart raced like the winner of the Kentucky Derby; his breaths rasped in and out of lungs that felt as though they were being wrung dry, and his blood flooded his veins like lava spewing from a volcano.

And this volcano was about to blow.

He had some concerns about the plan. Mainly whether or not he could control himself once they got naked. The thought of Ren touching herself in front of him just about had his eyes crossing; it certainly had his cock hard as granite and leaking pre-cum. Fuck knows what would happen when it was a reality —within touching distance.

God. He couldn't be in the same room as her. He'd never keep his hands off her.

The bed in the master bedroom faced the door. He could stand in the hall, lean against the wall opposite; with the door open he'd have a clear view of her.

"Ready?"

Ren's voice snapped him straight, sent the pounding in his body to deafening decibels. He turned slowly, his gaze meeting hers. Relieved to see her twisting her hands in front of her and the way she chewed the side of her bottom lip, he swallowed around the lump in his throat and attempted to speak. When all he could manage was a croak reminiscent of a dying frog, he nodded and tried to offer a reassuring smile.

He was pretty sure he failed.

She eyed him for a few seconds then without a word, turned and left the kitchen. He could hear her footsteps as she made her way to the bedroom. Just the thought had his cock pulsing, his breathing ragged, and sweat popping out all over his skin.

Taking a couple of seconds to gain control and hopefully stop the trembling in his legs, Brady wished they hadn't spent over a decade apart. If he'd stayed in Whispering Springs, they would have reached this point long ago. It would have been simpler. They would have gone from being best friends to mates without too much trouble.

Now they were strangers but not. And he'd hurt Ren by not contacting her. With hindsight he knew if he'd tried and succeeded, she never would have revealed his whereabouts or that she was talking to him. He could—*should*—have trusted her with that.

He'd allowed his mother to separate him from the one person he'd been most connected to. Shaking his head, he cleared it of the past and focused on the now.

Nothing stood in the way of them being together except Ren's reluctance. And that was wearing down. Slowly, with each minute they spent together, she let down her guard a little more and he knew they were growing closer, could feel the connection they'd always had weaving into place, the threads stronger than before.

"Brady?"

Sucking in a breath, he called out, "Coming," as he stripped out of his clothes and dropped them on the floor at his feet. Quick strides had him down the short hallway and at the bedroom door.

The vision before him buckled his knees, and he had to grip the doorframe with both hands to keep from falling to the floor. "Fuck."

Pillows piled up behind her back, Ren reclined against the headboard. Her full breasts—and god did she have a first-class rack—were on display, their red-brown tips hard and pointing his way. She'd bent her knees, widened her feet, and opened her thighs until everything was on show. Every wet luscious inch.

"*Fuck*," he breathed out harshly. His fingers dug into the timber frame, and he was relieved to see his claws hadn't extended.

The smile she gave him said she knew the power she held over him. They might both be virgins but that didn't mean they were clueless, and Ren definitely wasn't clueless. She knew exactly what she was doing to him when she trailed her hands down her torso, up the inside of her thighs to her knees, then back down again.

Her fingertips skimmed either side of her pussy, back over her stomach, and finally across those sweetly puckered nipples he wanted to wrap his lips around.

And then she did it again. Stroked her fingers over her quivering belly, skimmed the wet flesh between her legs, down to her knees before reversing once more.

Slowly she touched herself. Taunted him with what he couldn't touch. What he wanted to touch more than he wanted to breathe. When she started her third round of caresses, the pounding in Brady's head began to sound like a chant.

Take her, take her, take her.

Blood surged, pulsing through his body and stretching his cock to bursting in a throbbing beat that echoed in his ears, accompanying the words in his head—his soul. He wanted to claim her. Needed to.

Sweat coated his skin and he could feel the fine hair all over his body thicken to fur as his coyote howled to take what was his. With a clenched jaw, Brady removed one hand from the doorframe and wrapped it around his pre-cum slicked shaft.

He'd dripped on the floor between his feet. The puddle grew as he stroked his flesh in a slow, light caress. He didn't want to go off too soon, and if he grabbed his dick and fucked his hand the way he longed to, it would be over in seconds. Already his balls were tucked up tight and the tingle of eminent release tickled his groin. They needed to get this party started or he'd be partying alone.

"*Ren.*" Brady squeezed the base of his cock in an attempt to stem the tide. "I can't... I need... *Please.*"

Her eyes were glued to his hand, to the thick shaft gripped tight in his fist. Watching her, Brady saw the shiver that rolled over her, saw the slick folds of her pussy grow plumper, redder, wetter.

Before he could beg more, she slid both hands between her legs. One set of fingers spread her pussy lips wide and the other delved between to swirl around her clit. He could see the bud standing tall at the top, could see the opening of her channel fluttering with each stroke of fingers on clit.

Breathing ragged in his ears, it took him a moment to realize Ren breathed just as harsh, that her heart pounded as hard as his. She might look relaxed lying back on the bed except for the flushed glistening skin, the taut peaks of her breast, the rapid rise and fall of her chest, the plump red flesh under her fingers...

Yeah, she was right on the edge with him.

He could smell her. The rich scent of her arousal intensifying with every second, every breath—every stroke. Her hips were moving now, lifting off the bed as she thrust a finger deep inside.

His cock pulsed, jerked, and he took a half-step forward before he could stop himself. He couldn't jump her. She'd offered him this and he'd take it no matter how much effort it took to stay by the door.

She hadn't said anything since she'd called him and he had to think she was as wound up as him and incapable of uttering a word.

Words might not be flowing from her lips but that didn't mean she was quiet. No. She made the most erotic sounds. Little whimpers and moans as she thrust a second finger deep while strumming her clit with her thumb; the whole time she held herself wide open for him to see every detail, every pulse of her folds as more blood rushed to the area.

Brady groaned, clenched his jaw, and fought to keep his eyes open and his orgasm from exploding. With the number of times he'd jacked off in the last few days, it was a wonder he could get it up, never mind come. It could be the mating bond or the woman on his bed; either or both could be responsible for his constant arousal and hair-trigger.

"Brady," she moaned, her hips undulating faster. "I'm going to..." Pulling her bottom lip between her teeth, she threw her head back and exposed her vulnerable neck, making his teeth drop.

On a gasping cry she went over the edge, her body shuddering and quivering, her back arching as the waves of her release took her under.

He held off as long as he could so he could watch every second of her orgasm except his coyote had other ideas, and as he own release exploded, it blew everything wide open. His coyote had never been this connected to his human side before.

It was as though finding his mate pulled that primitive part of him closer to the surface, gave them a shared goal, and right now that goal was to claim their mate.

Only he couldn't.

It didn't matter how much he wanted to or that he knew he could take her without a fight; he couldn't break her trust. He'd promised to hold back. Go at the pace she set.

And if he was going to do that, he had to leave.

Had to get away from the one thing he wanted most.

Pain sliced deep. Neither he nor his coyote wanted to go

but if he didn't, he'd be on her. Marking her. Biting her. Claiming her.

With a roar, Brady emptied the last of his cum on the floor at his feet and spun around. Bouncing off the walls, he staggered back to the kitchen and the door that led outside.

"Brady!"

Ignoring Ren's call was the hardest thing he'd ever done, but he made it to the back door and flung it open. From one step to the next he shifted, let muscle and bone stretch and snap, reshaping him into the four-legged animal he was at his core.

Paws pounded on wood as he ran across the porch and launched himself into the snowy night.

"Brady!"

She'd followed him. With a quick glance over his back, he barked, growled a warning, before tearing off into the trees at the edge of the yard.

He hoped she wouldn't shift and follow him. He'd take her if she did. Neither of them would be happy about that. Their first time should be in human form. They could mate as coyotes after they'd sealed their bond, after their mating was complete and they'd claimed each other.

Pushing hard, he followed the trail he'd traveled over the last five days, winding his way through the trees until he reached the little creek at the base of the small incline the house had been built at the top of.

He'd done minimal exploring of the forest since he arrived. The house had taken most of his days but he'd made time to run every day. It settled him, to shift to his animal form and run free. Hopefully, running would calm the roiling hormones and urges of the mating bond.

Brady snorted.

Yeah, right. Nothing would soothe a mating bond except a mate. And his didn't want him.

No, that was a lie. She did want him; her body couldn't hide her true feelings, except she was reluctant to give in to their mating. Their history kept her guarded, more so than if they were strangers. He needed to give her time, needed to earn her trust and love once more.

As his muscles quivered and snow melted on his coat, Brady hoped it didn't take too long. He wasn't sure he could handle another session of exploring sex without touching her. If she wouldn't accept his mating claim, maybe he could convince her to accept his mark.

12

KAT WATCHED Brady disappear into the night. She'd heard the warning in his bark; he didn't want her to follow, and she wouldn't. But she wasn't going to leave him out there alone.

Heading back to the bedroom, she redressed, then cleaned up the mess Brady left on the floor, before making her way to the front door to grab her coat and boots. Pulling her gloves from her coat pockets, she slipped them on as well as her beanie. Checking the slide bolts on the front door were locked, she went back to the kitchen and pulled out the ingredients for hot chocolate.

She'd need something to keep her warm while she waited and Brady would need warming up when he got back.

The kitchen was clean. They'd taken care of that before they'd... Kat shivered.

Jeez. She'd never felt anything like what they'd done. Sure, she'd taken care of herself over the years; it usually took far longer than it had just now, but still, she'd known she wasn't frigid in spite of her lack of arousal with any of the men or boys she'd messed around with in the past.

She'd heard a mating bond could be intense. Gordie had been honest about her mating with Anthony all those years ago but that hadn't been a true mating like she had with Brady. And Kat hadn't thought about asking her sister about the bond with Steve. Not with everything else going on in recent weeks.

Gordie would be honest with her though. She could trust her sister's thoughts and opinions because she'd never lie to Kat.

Glancing around, Kat spotted her phone on the counter, and grabbing it, shoved it in her pocket. She'd get a cup of hot chocolate, the quilt from the bedroom, and head out onto the back porch to wait for Brady.

Plan set, she made quick work of heating the milk, adding the cocoa, and stirring until the liquid was smooth. She filled a mug, left the rest in the pan, then ducked into the bedroom to grab the quilt.

Back in the kitchen, she picked up her cup and headed outside into the cold. Slipping out the back door, she shivered as the wind buffeted her. Small flakes of snow caught on the swirling wind wet her face and she looked for the most sheltered section of the porch.

The only place to sit was an old swing that didn't look as though it would hold her weight, except it was out of the flying snow, and unless she wanted to huddle on the floor, her only option. Walking over she put her mug down, and gingerly lowered herself, slowly letting the seat support her.

When the chains didn't creak or groan, she figured it was safe. Bending over, she lifted her mug and sat back. Slipping her phone out of her pocket, she draped the quilt over her legs and tucked it around her waist.

Three taps had Kat connecting to her sister.

"Hey, what's up?" Gordie answered on the second ring.

"Hey." Taking a deep breath, Kat dove right in. "What was your mating bond like with Steve?"

"Whoa. Whoa. Where did that come from?"

"I need to know if this is normal."

"If what's normal? Kat, where are you? What's going on? You sound like you're outside in the storm."

Sighing, Kat started at the beginning. "Brady's my mate."

"I know. You told me, remember?"

She'd forgotten that. So much had happened since Brady arrived in town. "I'm at his house."

"Oh. Did you mate?"

"No. I'm not ready for that. We haven't even kissed."

"Then what has you all worked up? I know you, you're freaking out over something. Is it because you can't control this?"

"Yeah, I guess that's part of it. I asked him to wait. I don't want to mark each other or mate yet and, well, I suggested we fool around with ourselves in front of each other and we did, except something happened and Brady ran, shifted, and took off into the forest."

"Slow down, slow down, one thing at a time. Let me get this straight, you masturbated in front of each other so you wouldn't be marked; is that right?"

"Yes."

"Okay, that sounds like a normal thing to do whether you're a mated pair or not, and it's probably sensible until you can come to terms with the hurt you both suffered when he left Whispering Springs. So what happened that made Brady run?"

"I don't know! That's why I'm calling you! God, Gordie, he couldn't get away quick enough and he growled at me when I followed, the message to stay put perfectly clear. Did I do something wrong? We both got off and I thought we both enjoyed it but maybe—"

"Hang on a sec, Kat," Gordie ordered before her voice muffled. She could hear her sister talking to someone and assumed it was Steve. Gordie's next words confirmed it. They also confirmed that Steve had heard every word of their conversation so far. "I'm putting you on speaker so Steve can talk."

Kat groaned as she closed her eyes and leaned her head back. The action made the swing rock beneath her and she straightened—braced—ready for the thing to collapse. Nothing happened though, so she eased back into her reclined position and took a sip of cocoa.

"Kat?"

"Hmm..."

"Sorry to interrupt but I think I can shed light on what went on," Steve explained.

"Okay."

"It's my opinion, and Doc agrees with me, that Brady came close to claiming you without your consent. Now I don't know him, didn't before, and I haven't even laid eyes on him since he returned so I can't make a judgement call on his character but I can tell you what it sounds like. Gordie has told me a little about him in the last few days, and I trust her assessment of him. He's taken the immediate danger, danger as he perceives it, away from his mate. From you."

"He took himself away because he thought he'd hurt me?" Kat didn't understand how Brady could hurt her; he'd never be physically violent with her and she was sure he loved her and wouldn't be emotionally abusive either. Gordie had been right to point out Brady was nothing like his father or brother because he wasn't. He'd only ever been kind, caring, and protective.

"By claiming you before you're ready, he'd be hurting you. And him."

Steve's words lit up all kinds of light bulbs. "Oh."

Jeez, she was such an idiot.

Brady would never try to control her. He'd value her opinions, her wants; he'd even pushed his own wants aside to give her hers.

"Kat?"

"Yeah."

"He'll come back," her sister said.

"Yeah, he will." Taking a deep breath, Kat asked the question she was pretty sure she knew the answer to, but wanted to hear the words from Gordie anyway. "Will this be a problem for you, Gordie?"

"What? You and Brady being mates? Why would that be a problem for me?"

"Because he's a Connelly. I'll be living in the Connelly home." Oh God, when had she made that decision? "He'll be a constant reminder of what happened."

"The only thing Brady will be is the man who makes you happy. Who helps you give me lots of nieces and nephews to spoil."

Kat laughed. "Jesus, you two need to give me nieces and nephews first."

"We could do it together," Gordie whispered. "Mum and Dad would be over the moon if we did."

"I'm not even mated yet. Shit. We haven't even kissed."

"Then when he gets back, kiss him."

Kat didn't think they were ready for that but couldn't deny the desire was strong. There was something else she needed to ask her sister. "Hey, Gordie, do you remember Mrs. Connelly being pregnant?"

"No. I didn't live here when Brady was born."

"I mean when you were about nine."

"Nine...? No, I don't remember her ever being pregnant. Kat, what's going on?"

"You transferred all Dad's old medical records to digital form, right?"

"Yes, you helped. Why?"

"So if there was another Connelly boy, it would be recorded in Dad's files and you'd have put them in your database."

"Kathren Joy Monroe, you tell me right this second what the hell this is about. There's only two Connelly children that I know of, and I'm pretty sure I would have remembered seeing a record showing Mrs. Connelly having another baby whether the baby lived or not, and I don't."

Kat could hear the frustration and curiosity in her sister's voice. She owed it to her to explain, especially seeing how she was going to ask to see those records. "We found a birth certificate for Jacob Connelly in Brady's mom's things."

"Jacob? It doesn't ring any bells. And I've got a good memory."

"Brady said that."

"So you want me to search the files?"

"I was going to ask to do it."

"I'd let you but patient confidentiality has to be considered."

"I'm only asking to see Michelle Connelly's records and she's dead. Believe me, I have no intention of gossiping about what I find at the Den or anywhere else."

"Okay, if Brady agrees, yes, you can go through her file. When?"

"After the snow lets up?"

"I'll be at the clinic as soon as that happens, so come in whenever, and I'll set you up in the office."

"Thanks, Gordie."

"What are you thinking?"

God, her sister knew her too well. "I'm not sure yet but

something doesn't sit right with Brady's mom leaving Marcus behind. I can't pinpoint what, but it doesn't jive with the woman I remember."

"Yeah, I never understood that either and if I'm honest, I actually thought Malcolm had killed her and Brady, and hidden it. That was why I left after the accident. I don't remember it, anything, until I came to in the hospital but I always got a bad feeling around Malcolm and I had the nightmare where I was trapped and could hear him laughing."

"You never told me about that. But I know what you mean about Malcolm, he always gave me the creeps even before I had that run-in with him after Brady left." She didn't have the right to tell her sister Brady's revelation about the Wilders. He'd have to be the one to share that if it was going to get out. And she wasn't ready to voice her suspicion about her sister's accident either. So many things were clicking into place for her. For Brady's sake, Kat hoped she was wrong about most of them.

"Do you want to stay on the phone until Brady gets back?" Gordie asked.

"No. I'm good. I'll talk to you later."

"Message me every day."

Kat laughed. "I'm fine. I'll *be* fine."

"I know. I just worry with you being at the Connelly place."

"The threat the Connelly place held is long gone; you saw to that."

"I think there's more damage those men can do from the grave."

"What aren't you telling me?"

"Nothing."

"Bullshit."

"Right back at you."

"Fine. We'll keep our secrets for now."

"Secrets always find their way out into the open."

"They do, but these aren't mine to tell."

"Okay, let Brady know there's no rush on making a decision. He's got time."

"I think we should put that decision off indefinitely."

"Why?"

"You might want to do some research." God, she hoped she didn't give anything away. But her sister was good at reading between the lines, finding the pieces and putting the puzzle together. It was one of the many things they had in common. "Just don't do anything yet."

"All right."

Kat thought about the journals inside, the secrets they held, the one she thought might strip away everything Brady believed about himself and the family he'd been raised in.

"Call if you need me," Gordie said. "Any time. Day or night."

"Thanks. Give Steve a hug for me."

"Already on that," Gordie said with a laugh.

"'Night, Kat." Steve's deep voice reminded Kat she hadn't only been talking to her sister.

"'Night. And thank you."

"You're welcome. If he's not back in a couple of hours, give us a call. I'll head out and see if I can round him up."

"No need. I'm sure he'll be back when he's ready."

"Don't stay outside waiting too long, Kat; it's going to get cold fast," Gordie warned. "You can wait inside just as well as out there."

"How do you know I'm outside?"

"Do you even have to ask?"

Kat chuckled. "No. 'Night, you two."

"'Night," they chorused.

She disconnected and lowered the phone to her lap, her gaze on the dark shadow of the trees lining the yard.

She'd give Brady another ten minutes, then she'd go back inside. She doubted she'd be able to sleep until he returned but she could make herself useful while she waited. If the snow kept up, and it was supposed to, they'd be housebound for a few days, and nothing beat a nice pot of homemade soup on snow days.

She'd brought plenty of fresh vegetables with her earlier. The steak she'd brought would be better for stew but the whole chicken would make a nice accompaniment to all those veggies.

The wind howled through the trees, snow flying in every direction. Shivering, she tucked the quilt up under her chin.

It really was getting colder. Deciding Gordie had a point and not wanting to worry her or Brady if he came back and found her shivering on the back porch, Kat stood, gathered the quilt and mug, and headed inside.

13

BRADY SLIPPED in through the back door and cursed his own stupidity.

He'd left Ren alone. And she'd been forced to leave the door unlocked for him. He would have known if she were in danger but he should never have left her in such a vulnerable position.

Seeing his clothes folded neatly on the kitchen counter, he snatched up his underwear and t-shirt. He wouldn't need the jeans or sweater; it was long past time for bed, a bed he hoped he'd find Ren in.

Unless she'd risked the storm and gone back to town.

Making his way through the house, he checked everything was locked up and made sure the fire was banked before heading to the bedroom. He couldn't stop himself from crossing his fingers and whispering, "please be there, please be there," as he walked.

He hadn't abandoned her but couldn't—wouldn't—blame her if she saw his run into the forest as that. He'd barely held on to his control and he was ashamed he'd needed to, and proud he'd had the strength, to take himself away from her.

The mix of conflicting emotions he'd experienced since he'd arrived in Whispering Springs kept growing.

He hadn't expected his return to be easy but even those thoughts hadn't prepared him for the roller coaster of emotion he'd been on since he'd driven in to town. And if his worst fears were realized, the ride was far from over.

One thing kept him grounded, gave him a glimmer of hope that he'd make it through what was to come.

Ren.

And there she was. Curled on her side facing the door, snuggled beneath the quilt.

Brady took a moment to absorb the sight. In spite of his optimism, there had been a little niggle of doubt that he'd find her still here.

"Hey." Her sleepy voice brought his eyes to hers.

He smiled. "Hey."

She pulled the cover behind her back and murmured, "Come to bed. We can talk about it in the morning."

He walked closer but didn't climb in beside her. "I'm sorry."

"Nothing to be sorry about. You did the right thing. Now get in here and get warm. I doubt that cup of hot chocolate is still hot."

Brady spotted the mug on the side table. "You made me hot chocolate?"

"Hmm..." Her eyes drifted shut. "If you want I can reheat it."

"No." Brady circled the bed and slipped onto the mattress behind her. "I'd rather get warm by holding you."

"Can you do that without losing control?" she questioned with a sleepy slur.

He nestled in close. "Yeah, I think so. I'm more settled since we did what we did. Plus I'm exhausted."

"You've been gone for hours."

"Didn't go far."

"You could have locked yourself in the bathroom."

"No lock."

"Really?"

He grinned. "You didn't try to lock the door at all today?"

"No. Why would I. The door was closed."

Brady's grin widened. Yeah, she might not think she trusted him, but she did. It might not be a conscious thought but deep down she trusted he would respect her boundaries even if it were a simple closed door that she'd put between them.

Now he just needed her to trust him completely. He wanted everything with her and he knew he wouldn't get any of it until she believed in him—them—fully. "Go back to sleep. We'll talk in the morning."

After a few moments, she whispered, "I spoke to Gordie."

He hummed in answer. The long run and freezing temps he'd subjected himself to were catching up with him quickly.

"She doesn't remember your mom being pregnant or reading that she was in the files she transferred to the new database. She said we can take a look at your mom's file whenever we want."

"Mm'kay." Brady snuggled in behind Ren. "Sleep now."

"'Night." She wiggled back, her ass rubbing his groin, making his cock twitch.

Holding his breath, he concentrated on not getting another boner. Having her warm sleepy body in his arms had him at half-mast as it was and with the soft swell of her ass pressing against him, his body was reacting in the typical way. Blood rushed, his heart raced, and the half-mast headed towards full.

One arm beneath her waist, one draped over her hip, Brady

kept his hands still and focused on her breathing, tried to match his to hers. Before long she drifted off, and eyes closed, he savored the feelings coursing through him.

This was what he'd waited for, why he'd never been tempted by any other woman; this one had laid claim to his heart—his soul—when neither of them were old enough to understand the depth or meaning of their connection.

He'd do anything to get them back to the pureness of their childhood friendship. He couldn't erase the mistakes, couldn't get back the time they'd missed, but he'd be damned if he didn't make the most of every second he had with her now.

With a sleeping Ren in his arms, he could finally relax, could think about the fact she hadn't run back to town after he'd disappeared into the forest. Could believe they'd find their way to the future they both deserved. The future his father and brother had tried their best to steal.

He'd had plenty of time to think while he'd been outside. He'd hit the small creek and followed the water for a few minutes before turning back. Racing up the incline he'd checked the house then returned to the creek. Over and over he'd run the course he'd set until the weather threatened to blind him.

Brady knew he'd been gone hours. His muscles ached, and his bones felt frozen to the marrow. Ren hadn't complained about the cold when he'd climbed in behind her, and with her warmth and the quilt tucked tight around them, his body temperature had already returned to normal.

One thing that had been in the forefront of his mind was the secrets he knew his mother's journals held. He'd face them, bring them into the open so they could find closure. And if they proved to be hurtful to someone else, they'd decide together—he and Ren—who needed to know.

He might hate the idea of keeping secrets, but he wouldn't

hurt someone if they wouldn't benefit from the knowledge. Some things were best left buried.

Nuzzling his nose into the back of Ren's neck, Brady breathed deep and filled his lungs with the scent of her. They'd start going through the journals tomorrow. For now he'd hold his mate close and dream of their future.

THE SMELL of bacon frying and coffee woke him. Reaching out, he slid his hand across the bed beside him.

Empty.

That explained the glorious scents flooding the house and making his mouth water and belly rumble.

Ren was up and in the kitchen.

How many nights had he dreamed of this? Or days. The want for her hadn't been confined to the darkness of night. He'd spent too many times to count thinking of her, wondering what she was doing, who she was with. She'd taken root in his head and heart, and the longer he'd spent away from her, the deeper his yearning went.

"Sleeping Beauty is awake." His gaze flew to the doorway where she leaned against the jamb, a smile on her face. "Hungry?"

"Definitely." Throwing off the covers, he swung his legs over the side of the bed. "Why didn't you wake me? I would have helped cook."

"Don't need help, and you got in late so I let you sleep late, but it's time to get up now. We've got books to read."

The reminder made him pause. He'd almost forgotten about the possible time bomb ticking in the living room.

Taking a deep breath, he stretched his arms above his head and relished the pull on his muscles. He should do a session of yoga to iron out the kinks his late-night run left in his body. Although he wasn't sure he wanted Ren to know he was into yoga. Most men lifted weights or ran miles; Brady preferred the flexibility and strength yoga delivered.

He'd taken plenty of ribbing over it in the past. He hadn't let the teasing get to him before except the thought of Ren thinking he was a wimp didn't sit well.

"What's that face?" she asked, pushing off the doorway and coming closer.

"Oh, I, um..."

"Spit it out. No lies, remember?"

With a sigh, he let his arms drop. "I was thinking about doing yoga to stretch after last night's run."

"Really? You do yoga?"

"Yes." He waited for the laughing to start.

"Cool. Mind if I join you or do you prefer to do it in solitude? Wendy likes to practice alone, says it breaks her concentration if she can hear someone else breathing, but I don't mind sharing space with someone else when I do it."

Okay. That wasn't what he'd expected. "I don't think I'd mind. Never had anyone to do a session with so I guess we'll find out." Smiling, he pushed to his feet and moved in front of Ren.

Without asking, he pulled her in for a hug. She smelled like bacon and eggs and coffee. Three of his favorite things on his favorite person. Morning didn't get any better than this.

"We're snowed in."

"Yeah?" Brady couldn't find it in him to be upset by that.

"We've had a foot of snow overnight and it's still coming down, although it has eased off since I got up."

"This storm front is supposed to last a couple of days, right?" The idea of being trapped with Ren didn't feel confining at all; if anything it felt freeing. They would be free of outside influences and could make the most of the alone time to get reacquainted.

"Another forty-eight hours of snowfall according to the sheriff's department."

"Are you okay with that? Being stuck here?"

She leaned back and pressed a kiss to his chin. "Yes. C'mon, let's eat."

Pulling from his arms, she led the way out of the room. It was then he noticed she wore a pair of his sweatpants and one of his hoodies. Containing his grin was impossible, so he let it fly and followed behind her.

He found breakfast already on the table in the dark dining room. He really needed to knock out more walls, open up the entire area. Steam rose from their mugs and the platters of food. There was enough to feed an army. Good thing Brady had always had a healthy appetite. "Now this, a guy could get used to."

"Make the most of it. Normally by this time in the day I'd be at the Den serving this up to whoever wanders in."

"Well, count me in as a wanderer. I'll be there every morning." He dug into the pile of bacon and scooped more than half of the crispy meat onto his plate. He sighed. "And this is cooked exactly the way I like it."

"Wasn't sure if you would want sunny side up or over easy so I scrambled the eggs." Ren smiled at him. "Coffee is yours. It's a better roast than the one I brought with me."

"It was what my mother used. I'm not really a coffee snob. As long as it's hot, I don't care."

"Good to know."

"So what's a day in the life of Ren like?" he asked before shoveling a forkful of eggs between his lips. "Hmm...these are good," he praised through his mouthful. "Really good."

"It's the cheese."

Swallowing, he asked, "Cheese?"

"Yep. A sprinkle of grated cheese just before the liquid hardens and you need to stir."

"Well, whatever it is, they're delicious. Thank you."

"For?" Ren picked up her mug and brought it to her mouth.

"Cooking breakfast. You didn't have to. I don't expect you to take care of me."

She shrugged. "I like to cook."

"You also like to take care of people. But who takes care of you, Ren?"

Smiling, she put her cup down and leaned forward. "Apparently, you, *mate*."

"You want me to take care of you?" He had to tread carefully here. One wrong step and she'd back up again, and he knew they were on the verge of consenting to the mating bond.

"Isn't that what mates do? Take care of each other?" She cocked her head to the side, one eyebrow raised. "Did you change your mind after—"

"*Never*." He shot out of his chair and leaned over the table until his mouth was inches from hers. Fuck, he wanted to kiss her. Wanted to press his lips to hers. Wanted to lick his tongue along her plump lower one before pushing his way inside. "I'll never change my mind about you. About us."

"Okay. Well then. We should finish breakfast, then get started."

"Started?" He jerked upright. Jesus. Did she mean... His cock went rock hard, bulging the front of his underwear and poking out the top. He could feel pre-cum ooze from the tip.

"Oh, no, I don't mean we should"—she waved a hand between them—"you know. I meant we should get to reading those journals. You said you wanted all of that in the past before we mated."

Brady ground his teeth, clenched his jaw, his fists. "And you want that? To wait until after?"

"I." Her mouth snapped shut. She licked those lips he wanted to get his mouth on. "No. Yes. I want to go through the journals and see what happens. I'm not going to fight against our connection any more, but I don't want to jump in either."

"Okay." He held himself still. Breakfast forgotten in front of him. "Okay. I can do that."

"I'm asking too much, aren't I?"

"No. No, I, um, just need a second." He pulled in a few deep breaths, focused on getting his raging libido back under control. Strangely his coyote wasn't making a sound. Maybe because the bastard knew he'd get what he wanted soon enough.

Brady smiled.

Yeah, they could both relax. Because by the time their forced confinement ended, he'd be mated with Ren.

14

"BRADY?"

"Yeah," he muttered while continuing to rummage through one of the boxes they'd pulled out of the attic. He wanted to be sure he had all the journals his mother wrote and thought she might have left some behind when she'd escaped the house years ago.

Kat waited for him to look up. It took a few minutes but she wanted to have his full attention when she told him what she'd just read.

He pulled out a string of tangled lights and sighed. "Why would they keep these? They're obviously useless." He tossed them aside to join the growing pile of trash and dug back into the box.

"Brady." She slapped her hand on the timber floor.

"What?" He glanced up, a scowl on his face.

Something in her expression must have given him a clue because he pushed the box away and moved on his knees across the floor to where she sat, one of his mother's journals in her hand, the rest spread around her in date order.

"What? What is it?" he asked, his eyes on hers.

"Have you ever read any of your mother's journals?"

He shook his head but his eyes never left hers. "No."

"Not even when you were little and found one?"

"No. She hid them. At least that's what she told me. I didn't even know she kept them until she got sick."

"Oh. Right. Yeah, I can see why she'd hide these," she muttered, glancing down at the open page.

"Why? What's in them?"

God. How did she tell him? Should she tell him or make him read the words in his mother's hand? "Um..."

"Kathren, please. Just tell me what has put that look on your face."

Taking a deep breath, she thought about the best way to upend his life. And it would upend it. What was written in these journals would change everything he knew about his mother and father. About the brother whose body he'd come home to claim.

"Ren?" Brady grabbed her forearm, his fingers curling around and squeezing. "Whatever it is can't be worse than your father trying to destroy a whole town."

She smiled. "Not the whole town. Only the non-bloods and half-bloods."

"See? What could possibly be worse?"

Fuck. It was worse. So much worse. "I think you should read this part." She turned the journal she'd been reading and held it out, open to the page that would probably be the hardest to read. At least it was what she thought was the most shocking of what she'd read so far. Her eyes scanned the rest of the journals.

God. What else was in them?

"You can't tell me?" he asked as he took the leather-bound book.

Remaining quiet, she kept her gaze on his face, waited for him to look down and read the words that had been like a punch to her gut and they weren't even about her.

"Fine. I'll read it." But he didn't. His eyes stayed locked with hers for a long time before he took a deep breath and blew it out in a rush. "You could just tell me…"

Kat rolled her lips between her teeth and tried to keep her emotions at bay. It was hard though. This would hurt Brady. Hurt him in a way she wasn't sure he could recover from.

He hadn't given her the full details of the night his mother had taken him away or how it had affected him, but she'd got the impression it had scarred him deeply. This would open up those old wounds and deliver more.

Brady's voice cut through her thoughts.

"He brought the first child home the year I lost the fifth baby.
I didn't ask any questions. I should have asked questions.
The little boy was around two, barely talking or walking.
He cried. Cried for a mother I knew nothing of.
Malcolm told me to keep him quiet. To keep him out of sight.
I wasn't sure what had happened or why this little boy was here.
Matthew told me to be grateful. To mother the child as my own.
And as much as it shames me to admit, I didn't argue. I
accepted.
That boy became mine.
Became Marcus."

BRADY'S GAZE snapped to hers. "What the fuck?"

"I don't know." The confusion in his eyes matched her own. "I haven't read past that page. I didn't think I should…"

"You should. Jesus, I've got nothing to hide from you." He glanced down at the book in his hand. "But it appears as though my mother had something to hide."

"It sounds like your father and whoever Matthew is had a lot more to hide."

He took a deep breath and began to read again.

"In the first few years I kept to myself, to the house in the mountains.
No one came to visit in all that time. And I never ventured into town.
Not that Malcolm would have let me. He and Matthew brought supplies.
I was more a servant than wife and I was never the latter legally. But that's a story for another time."

"FUCK." Brady dropped the book to the floor and dragged his fingers through his hair.

She gave him time. Let him get his thoughts together before asking the question burning on her tongue.

"Did you know Marcus wasn't your blood brother?"

He shook his head. "No." His gaze met hers. "And now I have to wonder if I'm blood related to my parents. Marcus clearly wasn't."

Kat could understand why he'd think that. She wanted to know the answer herself. But she wanted so much more than that, and Michelle's journals held the answers.

"I think someone needs to read everything your mother wrote. I think..." she licked her lips, swallowed. "I think we might find out why your father wanted to destroy this town and why Marcus helped him."

"Why? It's not like they can be punished for what they did or understanding their motives will make anything better."

"No, they can't be punished. Death did that. As for making things better... Brady, there are secrets here that could answer a lot of questions people have, could help the town recover from the years of terror your father and his supporters subjected us to."

"He's gone now. He can't hurt anyone from the grave."

"But he can. His actions have left a taint on this town. It's dark and insidious and will continue to eat at us until we put it to rest."

Brady laughed but there was no humor in the sound. "Sure. Why not blacken the Connelly name more?"

Kat bit her tongue except it wasn't enough to stop her from voicing the words swirling in her head. "You might not even be a Connelly. Marcus wasn't."

"Fuck." He dragged both hands through his hair again, tugged the ends. "How do we do this? Shit, we need to tell the sheriff. The sovereign and regal, the council."

"Not yet." She put a hand on his arm in the hope of grounding him. His need to run was written all over his face and while she could see the appeal, the weather didn't allow for it. "I think we should read as much of these as we can before we do anything, say anything."

"Okay, okay. We'll see what other shit the Connellys did." He snatched up the journal and flipped the pages to the beginning. "I'll read this one. You grab another one."

"I've read part of that one so let me keep going. Do you have a pen and paper? I'd like to make notes."

"We should try and put them in time order."

"I've done that already. Can you get a pen and paper?" He needed something to focus on besides the thoughts spiraling in his head.

She let go of his arm except before he could get up, she threw her arms around his neck and pulled him close. Neither of them spoke. They sat on the floor for long minutes while Brady calmed and Kat comforted.

"Thank you for doing this with me."

"It's what mates do, right? Support each other."

"You still want to be my mate after what we just read?" he asked, his lips brushing against her neck where he'd burrowed in. "I wouldn't hold it against you if you didn't."

"You know me better than that, Brady."

He sighed into her neck. "Yeah, I do."

"I'll be here no matter what."

"God, I hope so because I don't think that's the only rotten skeleton we're going to find."

Kat didn't agree with him verbally; she didn't have to. They both knew if Malcolm Connelly was capable of taking a child and passing it off as his own, he was capable of so much more. What, remained to be discover.

She only hoped it didn't break Brady.

KAT MADE notes about the last two pages she'd read. It had taken a couple of hours but she was pretty sure she now understood what Malcolm and Matthew had been doing. She also understood that Brady's mother had been brought to Whispering Springs against her will. Turned against her will. The woman had been trapped in a situation she had no clue how to get out of or where to go for help.

Michelle Watson had been taken off a street in Omaha,

Nebraska, when she was barely eighteen. She'd been subjected to beatings and rape—because no one would argue otherwise—for years. All at the hands of a man who claimed to be her husband—her mate.

Kat still wasn't sure who Matthew was; Michelle hadn't mentioned a last name so far but she had mentioned him every time she wrote about the beatings. Up until this point he hadn't been involved in the rapes except the man had to have known what Malcolm was doing to his *mate*. Kat had no idea if Matthew was alive or not, but if he was she had every intention of hunting him down and putting him down.

No man deserved to live after what he'd done and allowed to be done to others.

It was the children that concerned Kat the most. They were under the age of three according to Michelle. So far Kat had a list of four names—names the men who'd kidnapped them had given them—and none of them were called Jacob.

Michelle knew nothing of where they'd come from before Malcolm arrived at the house with them. One thing Kat hadn't discovered, and what Michelle didn't seem to know up to this point in her journals, was where the children went after they spent a week locked in the shed out back.

The thought of going out to that shed had Kat's stomach clenching. Except she knew they would have to. Eventually. Maybe they would wait until they told the sheriff about what they'd uncovered.

Not that Brady had found much. He'd read half a journal before he dropped it to the floor and left the room. A few seconds later Kat heard banging from the back of the house. Wanting to be sure he was okay, she'd gone to check and found him taking out his anger on the wall dividing the back bedrooms.

She'd left him there. She knew someone who needed to be alone when she saw them.

That had been hours ago now.

Stretching her arms over her head, she dropped her chin to her chest then tipped it toward the ceiling, pulling on the kinks in her neck. It was time for a break. She'd make them lunch then decide what to do about the information she'd collected.

"Hey."

Turning her head, Kat found Brady in the doorway covered in dust and timber splinters. Smiling, she said, "You need to get cleaned up."

"Want some lunch? I'll wash up and make sandwiches."

"You wash up and I'll make something better than sandwiches." She'd brought a chicken pie with her yesterday that wouldn't take long to reheat.

"How'd it go?" Brady asked with a tip of his chin at the journals.

"Ah, I've gone through four so far. Do you know who Matthew is?"

"No. Should I?" His expression told her he didn't really want to know the answer to that.

"I don't know. He seems to be in every entry up to where I've read. You don't remember another man living here?"

He shook his head. "Was only ever Mom, Dad, Marcus, and me."

"Hmm..." Kat pushed to her feet. "Well, he's someone important in the early years of your mother's life here. I think he lived here too."

"Maybe you'll find why in a later journal." He eyed the leather-bound books warily. "I'll go wash up."

Kat watched him go with a heavy heart. Each thing she was discovering about Michelle Watson's past meant another scar for Brady. Not the physical kind, but the kind that were hidden, the kind that marked the heart and bled the soul. If what she was thinking was true, he'd be finding out he and Marcus had one thing in common.

Neither of them had been born with Connelly blood.

15

BY THE TIME Brady cleaned up and reached the kitchen, the most amazing aroma filled the house, making his mouth water and his stomach rumble.

He loved Ren for many reasons but her skill with food might top the list. His mother had always said the way to his heart was through his stomach.

His *mother*.

God, was she even his mother?

He'd always thought he took after her but now that he was questioning it, their looks weren't enough alike for there to be no doubt about his parentage. They had the same shaped nose and color eyes except that could be dumb luck over genetics.

Their hair was similar, except now that he thought about it, his mother's hair had been white blond where his was more dirty creek water blond. And the man he had considered his father until today had been a blue-eyed redhead but his brother —who wasn't his brother at all—had dark hair and dark eyes to go with his dark personality.

The more Brady thought about the family he'd been raised

in, the more he saw signs that all was not as it seemed. Marcus had never been happy. Even as a child, his brother had rarely smiled. And the number of dead animals he'd brought out of the forest over the years had to be excessive. Malcolm Connelly had always praised a kill, and Marcus had been pleased with both the praise and the spoils of the hunt.

Now Brady had to wonder if Marcus's need to kill hadn't been a big red flag his mother should have noticed. Then again, after recent revelations he didn't know or understand the woman anymore, so perhaps she'd been as pleased as her husband with their first son's efforts.

Except Marcus hadn't been their son.

And if Marcus wasn't, then what about him?

Hunting and killing had never appealed to Brady. Even in coyote form he didn't like to hunt. Maybe that was another sign he should take note of. So many things about his life he could no longer be certain of. So many questions and no one to answer them except a set of private journals left behind by the woman who'd raised him.

Shaking his head, Brady dispelled all thoughts of his family and the past, and brought his focus back to the woman in front of him. The one currently bent over at the stove.

She still wore his clothes and in spite of them being too big for her, the pants molded to the sweet curve of her ass as she leaned over and reached into the oven.

He opened his mouth to offer a hand but snapped it shut again. He didn't want to startle her in case she bumped into a hot surface. Instead he rested a shoulder on the doorframe and watched her lift a pie dish and place it on the counter. He couldn't help but admire her strength and ease as she worked. She was comfortable here, in the kitchen. He'd love to watch her at the Den.

It would be her place.

The one where she took control, held the reins, and directed others to do as she wanted.

"It's ready," she said without turning around. "Want to pour us coffee?"

Brady was one hundred percent sure he hadn't made a sound and she'd had her back to him the whole time; there was no way she would have seen him in her peripheral vision.

Frowning, he pushed off the doorjamb and asked, "How did you know I was here?" on his way to the coffee pot.

"I heard you leave the bedroom, could smell you when you came into the room." She glanced over her shoulder, her brow furrowed, her eyes squinting. "Actually, it was more that I sensed you than smelled you, but once I felt you behind me I could pick out your scent over the chicken pie."

"Mating bond." Grabbing the pot, he filled the two mugs she had placed on the counter beside the machine. "We might not have completed it or even marked each other but our connection is growing stronger."

"It is. Which is why I think we should mark each other after lunch," she casually tossed over her shoulder with a smile as if those words weren't the most significant of his life.

"Wh—" Saliva caught in his throat. "What?" he choked out. Coughing, he cleared his throat and asked, "You want to mark each other? After lunch?"

She'd fought against their bond long enough for Brady to believe it would be weeks before she would accept him and they could do anything about the connection strengthening between them with every second they were together, and now she was giving in? Just like that?

"What happened? What did you read in those books?" he demanded.

Something had to have triggered her acceptance. She'd said

she wasn't going to fight their attraction—connection—but this was taking the reins and... *Ah.*

"You want to be in control, and to do that you say when and how," he guessed.

Ren turned and faced him fully. "Yes and no."

"Explain it to me because this one-eighty has my head spinning." And his heart racing. He crossed his arms over his chest even though every instinct screamed to cross the damn room and pull her into his arms and against his chest.

"I'd like us both to be in control, to make active choices instead of reactive, and I want you to know that those journals, whatever they reveal about you, or your family, make no difference to the way I see *you*. The way I *feel* about you."

"We were going to put the past in the past first."

"The past is already in the past; it doesn't change the fact we're mates or that I want to be your mate."

"You said you didn't want to."

"No. I said I wasn't happy about being forced to mate. But, Brady." She took a step toward him making every muscle in his body clench, his lungs seize. "If I had to choose, out of all the men I've known in my life, I'd choose you. Every time. I *chose* you before I knew what it meant to be mates, before I knew what love was I *loved* you. When you left, it hurt and I wanted to blame you for that, and for everything your family has done to mine, but you aren't to blame for any of it. Yes, you should have come back sooner. Yes, you should have tried to contact me at some point over the last thirteen years, but I understand why you didn't."

"Glad one of us does."

She smiled at him. "You know why you didn't."

"Yeah," he sighed. And he did.

He'd been trying to please the one person he still had in his life, the woman who'd raised him and now might not even be his mother.

A growl rumbled in his chest. "I hate all the secrets."

"Then let's make a rule right now, one we live by for the rest of our days. No secrets between us. *Ever.*"

"I love you." He'd planned to hold back those words but if they weren't keeping secrets, then he needed to say them whether she reciprocated or not. He needed her to know he was all in.

Ren's smile grew as she closed the distance between them and placed her hands on his chest. "And I love you."

"Can we though? Love each other?" he wondered. "We haven't seen each other in years and we've both changed, grown. We don't really know each other anymore."

"Are you doubting what you feel or what I feel?"

He shrugged. "Both?"

"Okay, then let's agree we have strong feelings of *like* to go along with our mates bond and we're prepared to build on those."

"Then we shouldn't mark each other." Fuck. He couldn't believe he was thinking it, never mind voicing it. "We should wait until we're sure."

"I'm sure I want to be marked by you. If you don't want me to mark you yet, that's fine. I'll wait."

"*No.* I want that. I just..."

She slipped her arms around his waist and laid her cheek on his shoulder, her face tucking in to the side of his neck. "Brady, I'm not going to change my mind."

"You already have," he argued. "Not a week ago you ordered me out of the Den, and now you're inviting me to make the most intimate connection two coyotes can make."

"That wasn't about you."

"How could it not have been about me?"

Behind him she gripped fistfuls of his shirt and tugged. "It was about everybody else. All the crazy shit that's gone on in recent weeks, months. Jeez, years."

"And me."

Ren sighed; her warm breath bathing his neck sent ripples of goose bumps across his skin. "Yeah, and you."

"Then we should wait." God, he was an idiot who should bang his head on the nearest wall.

He had the woman of his dreams asking him to mark her, and he was trying to change her mind, put her off.

Damn. He wasn't an idiot, he was fucking insane.

"Do you think we would wait if we'd just met?" she inquired with a smirk in her tone.

Damn her. She had him. He tightened his arms around her. "No, probably not."

Would it be so bad to mark each other? He knew there was nothing that could possibly change his mind about Ren. She was it for him, had been his whole life, but then she wasn't the one with all the rotting skeletons in her family closet.

Anything could come out of his mother's journals. They'd already discovered Marcus wasn't born a coyote, wasn't a Connelly by birth. Most likely Brady wasn't either.

She held tight to his shirt, her arms banded around his ribs, squeezing as though she knew he needed something to ground him, while his mind spun in circles going over the same things again and again.

Holding her close gave him strength; it also gave him thoughts of being in this position naked.

It would be so easy to take her up on the offer, to pick her up and carry her to the bedroom where he could spread her out on the bed and explore every inch of her body.

A shudder went through him. "I don't know if I could stop myself from claiming you once we started," he admitted.

"Is that why you're backpedaling? You think I'll be upset if we complete our mating bond while marking each other?" She leaned away, her arms remaining locked around him, a frown on her face. "Brady, I think you misunderstood what I'm asking. Or maybe I worded it wrong. I think we should claim each other. Mark, sex, bite, the whole bonding thing."

If he thought his body had clenched before, it was nothing compared to right now. He was so tight it wouldn't surprise him to find he'd lost inches in height and width; his skin felt like it had shrunk two sizes, compressing muscle and bone.

Dragging air into his lungs, he pushed it out through strangled vocal cords. "Did you turn the oven off?"

Ren's forehead wrinkled, her nose scrunched up. "Yes, why —hey!"

He couldn't stop a smile from stretching his lips as he scooped her off the floor into his arms and made for the bedroom. If they were doing this—and god help him, they abso-fucking-lutely were—he would do it right, do his best to make it good for Ren.

Which meant he had to get her naked and leave his own clothes on. To begin with.

If he let his cock out now, the damn thing would be shoved inside her before either of them blinked. And Brady wasn't about to embarrass himself like that. He'd be sure to make her come and if he managed not to come in his pants while doing so, he'd jerk off so he wouldn't be on edge when he took her the first time.

Fuck.

He was about to lose his virginity to the only woman he'd ever wanted. When did his life get so great?

Only days ago he thought he'd be run out of town by an

angry mob, Ren leading the charge, and now he was lowering her to his bed, getting ready to sink inside her virgin body.

Double fuck.

There was no way he wasn't coming in his pants this first time.

16

BRADY'S HANDS curled around her waist, his grip sure—confident—before he skimmed them under her hoodie and up her ribcage. He hissed out a breath, his gaze darting to hers when he discovered what she wore beneath it.

"Fuck. No bra." His palms cupped and squeezed, fingers caressed and tweaked. "I need to see you."

He didn't have to ask twice. With a wiggle, she pulled the sweater up and bared her breasts.

"Jesus. Take it off." Slipping his hands behind her back, he lifted her up. "Take it all the way off."

Gripping the hem, Kat tugged the hoodie over her head and tossed it across the room where it landed in a heap on the floor.

"These too." Brady let her fall back to the bed and yanked on the waistband of her sweats, their fit so loose they were at her knees in one tug. "Jesus fucking Christ. No underwear at all? You've been walking around all day without anything under my clothes?"

"I didn't want to put my dirty—"

"Don't care." He slid the pants the rest of the way off and

threw them in the direction of the hoodie. "New rule. No underwear at home."

His fingers came back to her waist, trailed over her skin as he explored the area, the slightly abrasive pads delivering a sensation between tickle and caress. She shivered beneath his touch as his strokes swept lower down her torso.

Grinning, he said, "Yeah, I really like that rule."

"Goes both ways." Her breathing hitched, her insides clenched, as he concentrated on a particularly sensitive spot on her belly right above her mound. "If I don't get to wear them, neither do you."

"Agreed. No underwear for either of us from now on."

Smiling, Kat reached for the button on Brady's jeans. "Let's get yours off then."

His hands covered hers. "No. Not yet. I want this to last and if I get naked now, it's not going to."

Her gaze caught his. She could see his coyote just beneath the surface, felt his fingers tremble on hers. "You're close to shifting."

"I know."

"Should we mate in coyote—"

"Fuck no! The first time I have you, I want my hands on you. Your hands on me."

"Then..." She didn't know. Had no clue how to navigate the need visibly coursing through Brady. Her own coyote was happy to be on her back, offering herself to her mate. "Tell me what to do."

"Lie back and enjoy."

"But—"

"Shh..." One finger covered her lips as he leaned over her. "Let me make this good for you."

"I want to touch you too." Kat ran her hands up his sides,

over his chest, and around his neck. Locking her fingers together, she pulled his mouth to hers. "Kiss me, Brady."

Their lips met. A soft brush, back and forth. A little pressure. A lick of tongue.

They took their time, pressing, brushing, closed mouths learning the shape and feel of each other.

Kat had kissed boys. She'd kissed men. None of them kissed her the way Brady did. Like she was a treasure to be explored with a thoroughness that left her breathless.

His tongue stroked across her lips making them tremble, her breath sigh. He nipped at her top lip, bit into the bottom one with more force, and tugged before soothing the sting with the hot swipe of his tongue. He spent what felt like forever exploring her lips before pulling back enough to lock eyes with her.

"Open for me," he breathed against her mouth. "Let me taste you."

Parting her lips for him came as naturally as breathing. She wanted to let him in, wanted him to take whatever he wanted from her. To give him everything she was without fear or prejudice. It was just the two of them. No one else had a right to come between mates, and Kat vowed to make sure no one and nothing—past or future—did.

As his fated mate, her coyote had already bonded to his, but as a human she had the choice to give him her heart or guard it against any pain he could inflict. Except loving someone meant they could and would hurt you. That's what loving did.

It opened you up, bared you to the one you loved, and gave you the power to hurt and heal.

Kat intended to heal Brady.

"Take your clothes off."

Jerking away, he frowned at her. "I can't if I want to stay in control."

"I don't want you in control. I want all of you."

"You'll get me but I want to make it good for you first."

"Is this a macho-alpha coyote thing where you have to prove you can please your mate because I don't need that shit. Not between you and me."

"No. I don't want to hurt you, I want to make sure you're ready."

"I couldn't be any more ready, Brady. My thighs are slick with how ready I am. It's a wonder you can't feel how wet I am through your jeans."

"Ren. Please. I need to do it this way. Let me make you feel good then—"

"No. We do this together. I don't care if you get off quick because I can guarantee you I'll be right there with you." She cupped his face in both hands. "Brady, I need you inside me. And I don't mean your tongue in my mouth, although I'll take that too."

Air burst from his mouth and his eyes closed tight. "I'm afraid I'll go off the second I get inside you. That I'll be too quick for you to come."

"Then we won't stop. We'll keep going and from everything I know about a mating bond you'll stay hard. I'm not in heat, so I can't get pregnant, but I want to feel your cum inside me. I want to feel your warmth fill me up—"

"*Fuck!*" He dropped his chin, his breaths rushing in and out of his lungs in harsh explosions.

Before Kat could argue more, Brady levered up on his hands and sprang from the bed. At first she thought he would run like he had the night before but then he did what she'd asked and stripped.

And holy hell was she glad it was daylight and she could see every glorious inch of Brady Connelly in all his nakedness, because damn was he a sight to behold.

And hold.

She planned to do plenty of holding.

"Get back here," she demanded, spreading her legs wide in invitation.

A growl rumbled from his throat and his eyes lightened, his coyote showing through with the need to claim. "I don't want to mount you from behind in spite of everything in me demanding it. I want to see your face when I sink inside you."

"We can do the mounting thing next time."

Brady closed his eyes and shuddered. Pre-cum dripped from the tip of his engorged cock and Kat licked her lips.

What would he taste like? Would he let her lick him like an ice cream?

"*Kathren*," Brady growled, his voice rough and deep. "Eyes up here."

Dragging her gaze away from his groin, she found his hands clenched at his sides, the muscles and veins in his arms bulging. Further up, his chest heaved with each breath and his nipples pebbled within the light dusting of hair. The sharp angle of his jaw jutted forward, muscles clenching on both sides of his chin; his nostrils flared wide with each inhalation and his eyes blazed with a feral light that singed, caught fire beneath her skin.

Her coyote whined, whimpered in submission, and Kat had to fight the need to turn over, to offer him her back, turn her head, and offer her throat.

She could satisfy both her coyote and his if she gave him the latter so she twisted her head to the side, arched her neck to show him the tender sweep of her throat.

"Fuck. I'm done waiting." He lunged, caging her beneath him in one leap. "Open for me. Spread your legs and wrap them around my waist."

She was already lifting her feet, bending her knees, and curling her legs around him. Crossing her ankles, Kat locked her limbs around Brady's waist and raised her hips. "Don't wait. If there's any pain, get it over with quickly."

"No." He lowered his pelvis, pressed the length of his erection against her sensitive folds. "I won't hurt you."

"You might not be able to help it, Brady." She grabbed his face, made sure her gaze held his. "It won't last long and I doubt it'll be that bad. I've used a vibrator"—his eyes closed on a groan—"so it's not like I haven't had anything inside me before."

"Ren." His eyes snapped open, the fire in them scorching her from skin to bone. "Shut up. Stop talking. Let me think."

Rocking her hips up, she dragged her clit along his cock, over the tip, until the plump head rested at her opening. "Now. Brady."

"*Ren.*"

His protest came too late. Using her thighs, Kat rose up and took him deep. A spike of pain shot through her, a fiery flash that was there and gone in less time than it took to suck in a breath.

"Ren?" Brady cradled her head, laid his forehead on hers, and pressed his lips to hers. "Shit. Ren," he breathed against her mouth. "I didn't want to hurt you."

Drawing in a deep breath, Kat concentrated on the sensations rolling through her. "I'm okay."

"I hurt you."

"*We* hurt me." She needed him to understand that the pain had been worth it. To be joined with him like this, to feel him inside her, stretching her with his heat, to know neither of them had done this before, that they'd only ever do this together. "Brady, I promise you, it's already gone and it was minor. I've survived worse."

"What?" His head jerked up. "What worse? How worse?"

"Relax." She stroked a hand down his back. "The last time I sliced a finger at the Den hurt ten times as much."

He frowned. "I don't like the idea of you being hurt."

"We have that in common."

"No, really. I don't think you should use knives anymore."

Kat rolled her eyes. How he could focus on something other than their current position was beyond her. "Brady. You need to move."

His gaze met hers, gold sparking as his body's impulses began to take over once more. With a short jerk he pulled back, the drag of flesh on flesh drawing a moan from each of them. "Promise me," he demanded.

"What?"

"Promise you'll tell me to stop if it hurts."

God, how could she ever think this man would hurt her—physically or emotionally? He wouldn't. It wasn't in him to do it. He'd sooner inflict pain on himself than her. "You won't hurt me."

"*Promise me.*"

"I promise." She gave him what he needed. "I'll never lie to you. And no matter what happens we're in this together."

"I couldn't live if I hurt you again."

Kat slapped her hands on either side of his face. "Stop. It wasn't your fault. You'd never intentionally hurt me, Brady, I know that to the depths of my soul."

He lowered his brow to hers. "It would kill me," he breathed against her mouth.

"I know."

His breath rushed out. "I can't believe we're here." His hips flexed, pumping his cock in and out in a quick, short thrust.

She couldn't hold in the moan, not when pleasure snapped through her, pulsing and sparking and making her insides clench around his hard length. "Again."

"That didn't hurt?"

"God, no."

The pain had been nothing. There and gone and all that was left in its wake was a different kind of pain. The kind that drove you mad until the man you loved drove himself inside you.

"I need..." She rocked her hips, squeezed internal muscles, and had them both moaning.

The movement had Brady bucking, flexing, thrusting. Had him lowering over her further, had his breath hot in her ear as he nuzzled into her neck. "Fuck. It's too good."

Kat took that as a compliment; she didn't worry about the fact he had no reference to compare it to. This was them, would always be them. No one and nothing would come between them ever again.

She curled her back, tilted her pelvis so her pussy was in perfect alignment for Brady's cock. He drove into her, over and over and as his breathing became more shallow, faster, so did his thrusts. His body ground against hers, the pressure on her clit with each plunge quickly taking her up toward the peak she'd only ever reached on her own.

Sure, she'd used Brady to get there yesterday but she'd been the one touching her body, pressing deep and plying her clit until the inevitable happened.

Now it was Brady. Her mate. The man she'd loved when he was no more than a boy. They might not know each other as well as they had but it didn't stop her heart from spreading wider than her legs and drawing him inside.

"I'm going to..." Brady panted.

Kat smiled. "Don't stop." She reached between them, slipped her fingers around one taut nipple and pinched.

Light burst, sensation exploded, and Kat went over the edge with a cry.

She wasn't aware of her teeth dropping, of leaning forward to suction her mouth to Brady's neck and sink them deep. Caught in the maelstrom of pleasure, she screamed around the flesh between her teeth when Brady reciprocated.

Warmth spread inside her core, muscles clenching and flexing and gripping. Spasm after spasm had them rocking together, Brady driving deep, deep, deeper, until a final wave of ecstasy took them under.

17

PANTING FOR BREATH, Brady collapsed on Ren. Twisting to the side he took some of his weight off her but he couldn't bring himself to roll off completely.

He liked having her beneath him.

Her body cradled his in all the best ways and he loved how her pussy wrapped around his dick as though they'd been made to fit together forever.

He didn't have any idea what sex felt like with anyone except Ren and while that might not be every man's choice, Brady was extremely happy he'd waited. Ecstatic that she'd be his one and only. The fact he'd be hers only made that feeling multiply.

It wasn't as though he was some alpha asshole who wanted his woman pure or anything. He didn't. He wouldn't have been any less happy with his current situation if Ren had been with a hundred other men.

The thrill for him was in *her* being *his* only.

"Let's run."

"What?" Pulled from his thoughts, Brady raised his head and stared down at Ren. "You want to go for a run?"

"Yes." She pushed against his shoulders. "In coyote form."

"Um..."

"C'mon. Can't you feel it?"

Brady flexed his hips, his semi-hard cock still buried inside her. "Yeah, I feel it," he said with a chuckle.

Laughing she pushed at his chest this time. "Not that."

"You can't feel that?" He grinned down at her and rocked his pelvis back and forth. "Let me help you."

"Brady," she moaned. "I want to run with you."

The edge in her voice made him stop moving. "Why?"

"We never did before..." She pulled her bottom lip between her teeth, one lengthened canine showing. "I want to do this right."

"I don't think you have to worry about that. For a couple of virgins, I think we did it right."

"Not that!" she laughed, swatting at his arm with her hand.

Smiling, he lowered his forehead to hers. "Okay. You want to shift to coyote and run together. I get it. But Ren, it's still snowing."

"Oh." Her gaze moved to the window where the falling snow bumped against the glass.

"We should wait until after."

"After it stops?"

"No. After I take you again." He pulled his hips back then drove them forward. From root to tip, her pussy walls sucked at him, the slick heat making his half hard cock full to bursting in a single thrust.

He hadn't been worried, but when she arched up to meet him, when her walls clenched around him, Brady knew they weren't going for a run any time soon.

Lowering his head, he took her mouth in a hungry, wet kiss

that had him breathing hard and thrusting harder. His chest pressed to hers, the lush curves of her breasts pillowing his body, their hardened tips poking him.

They spent forever licking and rocking. Mouths and sex joined in a slow sensual climb to the top. With each stroke, each slide of flesh on flesh, the tension tightened, the need increasing until Brady was driving in, plunging deep with tongue and cock. Panting into her mouth he let his body lead him. Lead her.

She worked with him, followed him, led him, in their search for satisfaction. He might have done this for the first time only moments ago but he knew what he wanted, what to do. Knew how to make her want, how to make her feel good.

And right now his instincts drove him to mount her.

Pulling from her body, he grabbed her hips and flipped her over. The squawk that left her mouth was part displeasure, part surprise. Except she didn't have time to protest further because he dragged her ass up, spread her legs with his, and plunged deep once more.

"Brady," she gasped, her pussy clamping down on his length hard enough to bruise.

Her back bowed, her shoulders and head dropping to the mattress, her ass pressing into him more.

He grinned in triumph and hammered into her harder. Deeper.

Arching over her back, he kept one hand on her hip and slid the other around beneath her in search of her clit. When he found his prize, he used their combined slickness to ease the glide of his fingers and stroked the rock-hard bundle of nerves until she was bucking under him.

Her gasps and moans, the wet slap of flesh on flesh, an accompanying soundtrack to their claiming. He might be the one taking her—claiming her—but she was claiming him in return. With every sound, every movement, she owned him. Heart. Soul. Coyote.

Bent the way he was, he had a perfect view of his mark on her neck. Neither of them had said a word about the bite they'd each delivered. About the mating mark that now sat on both their necks. He didn't remember sinking his teeth into her, didn't remember anything except the blinding pleasure Ren's fangs had delivered the moment he'd let go.

His orgasm had been powerful but when her teeth had punctured his skin it had just about blown his head off, and right now, looking at his own bite mark on Ren's smooth skin, he wanted to do it again. Wanted to take them both to oblivion once more.

He used his hand on her pussy to hold her close and slid the other up her waist, over one breast to her throat. Palming that delicate column, Brady applied a small amount of pressure, his arm across her torso supporting her weight, pulling her into him.

"I'm going to bite you," he whispered into her ear. "Just like before, I'll sink my teeth deep and claim you as mine."

She shuddered against him, her breath coming in harsh pants. "Brady."

His name on her lips in that breathy little way sent a shaft of lust through his groin, made his cock pulse, his balls draw up tight, and he knew he didn't have much time before he fell off the edge. He wouldn't go there alone.

"Ren," he murmured, then tongued her ear lobe, grazed it with his teeth.

Her body clenched around his thrusting length, her slick walls tightening with each retreat as though she couldn't bear for him to leave her. She needn't worry. Brady had no intention of going anywhere that wasn't with her. Nothing in his life from now on would be done without Ren.

He nipped the side of her neck. "Tell me," he growled needing to hear her acknowledge his claim on her.

"I'm yours." She turned her head as much as his hold on her throat would allow and locked her gaze with his. "I've always been yours."

"And you always will be." Gripping her tighter, he picked up the pace, pounded a little harder, dove a little deeper. "I'll never let you go now that I have you."

"I wouldn't let you."

Brady could see the truth of her words in her eyes. He might be attempting to mark her soul so she'd never be rid of him but she would do the same in return. She'd leave him with no doubts about their mates connection.

Her gaze softened as she stare at him, her body pinned in place by his. "I love you, Brady. I've always loved you."

His eyes closed, his lungs drawing in a deep breath while his body continued to rock into hers. "Love you too. Always," he whispered against her ear right before he dragged his teeth down her neck.

"Do it."

Gaze on hers once more, Brady smiled. "You can't bite me in this position."

"Don't care. I'll bite your ass later." She bucked her hips against him, drove her ass into his next thrust with brutal force. "Bite. Me."

Canines dropping, he lowered his head and pressed his lips to her neck and the mark already there. He licked at each of the puncture wounds. Breathing her in, he took his time playing his mouth over the bite that would forever mar her skin.

The whole time he drove his cock into her, stroked her clit, and held her in place. Tension rose; her need for release, his need to claim, coiled in an ever increasing swirl of desperation.

And when she writhed against him, when her breath came

in panting bursts, her moans turning to whimpers and whines, he knew it was time to take them both over.

In unison, he drove deep inside her, bracketed her clit between his fingers and squeezed, and sank his fangs into his mating bite.

They exploded together.

A scream tore from Ren's throat, a hoarse groan from his, and their bodies thrashed and bucked with the waves of pleasure shooting through them.

Brady wasn't sure if they were both climaxing or if this was some kind of out-of-body thing because while he felt the ecstasy jolting through him, it didn't feel like his own; it felt like an echo of hers. His coyote howled in his head, the beast rippling beneath his skin, and his vision blurred, went white.

Flash lighting lit him up on the inside, scorched his veins and rose every hair on his body, the fine covering thickening with the shift threatening to take him over.

"Brady!"

Ren's cry brought him back to earth, her mad scramble beneath him snapping him out of his own mind and body to realize he wasn't the only one struggling against a shift.

He jerked back, ripping his body from hers in a brutal move that sent a shock of pain, a shaft of pleasure, through his groin. Disengaged, Brady sat back on his heels and watched Ren shift to coyote in front of him.

A grumbling whine echoed around them as she dropped to her belly, her tail curling around her hind leg, her muzzle flat on the bed, tongue out, breath panting.

"Fuck." Brady clenched his fists. His jaw. "Ren."

Her eyes met his, pleading. Confusion and pain swirled within the dark brown depths. He knew what he had to do.

Climbing from the bed, he ran for the back door and threw it wide; spinning around to get Ren, he found her behind him.

"Let's run." Shifting quickly, Brady led the way outside into the falling snow.

He shouldn't have ignored her earlier request. Shouldn't have taken her—bitten her—so soon after claiming her the first time.

Clueless as to the mating bond process, Brady should have known Ren's instincts were good. She'd wanted to run. He'd distracted her with more sex, another bite, and now they were in the woods, running between the trees at break-neck speed while snow drifted down around them.

Brady guided Ren down the slope to the creek then along the bank. They ran for long minutes, his coat wet from sweat and snow, before Ren barked and came to a stop. He didn't know why she'd stopped or what she had in mind, but he would let her lead on this.

She stood at the water's edge, her breathing labored, her coat shiny with dampness, and Brady had to struggle to pull air into his lungs. Not from their run. Physically fit, their dash from the house hadn't winded him, but the sight of Ren did.

Dark fur tipped with silver covered her coyote body. She wasn't small but she wasn't as big as him. It seemed strange that as humans they were around the same height but as coyotes he was at least a third bigger than her.

With a ripple of muscles, she shifted to human. "I'm sorry."

Changing quickly, on feet he stepped closer. "For what?"

"For losing control."

"Control?" he moved even closer. "You think I'm worried about you losing control with me? I want you to lose control. I want you to trust me enough to lose it but also to let it go. I need you to let me take care of you, and there isn't a more vulnerable state than when you give up or lose control."

"But—"

"No buts." He grabbed her hands, held them tight in his. "I

want to be the person you're the most comfortable with, the one you trust to catch you if you fall, the one who makes sure you're not in danger. I want to love you and be loved by you, but most of all I want you to know that if you lose control, if you let it go, I'll be right there to make sure you're okay. I want you to trust me to be there—*here*—right beside you."

"I do trust you." She stepped into him bringing their now cold bodies flush together. "I trust you with every part of me. But, Brady, I could have hurt you by shifting when we were..."

He laughed when she couldn't finish her sentence, when a blush rose up her throat and filled her face. "The most that could have happened is a few scratches and the interesting predicament of being caught inside you."

Ren's face scrunched up, a clear look of distaste in her eyes. "Eww..."

Laughing harder, he pulled her hands around his back and held them there. "Yeah, maybe."

She tried to yank free. "Gross. Brady that's disgusting."

"Nothing about you and me together is disgusting. I'm not saying I want to take you that way but if we found ourselves in the position again and I wasn't fast enough to pull free, it wouldn't be disgusting. It would be us and anything between us is neither disgusting nor off limits. As long as we're both enjoying what we do, or find ourselves doing, I'll think it's the most wonderful thing in the world."

Rolling her eyes, she muttered, "Great. I've hooked up with a freak."

"Ren, I shift into a coyote. Ain't nothing freakier than that."

"That's not freaky."

He arched one brow.

"Fine, some may find it a little weird."

"I'd think anyone who wasn't a coyote shifter would find it weird."

"Pretty sure wolf shifters don't think it's weird."

"Oh no, wolves are weird. I've met a couple." He chuckled. "Definitely weird."

"Speaking of weird…"

He knew what she was getting at. "We should go back to the house and figure out what to do about the journals."

"I think you need to tell the sovereign and sheriff. I thought we could ask Gordie and Steve to invite everyone to their place so we're on neutral territory."

"Not a bad idea." He held her close and took a deep breath. The scent of her—them—filled his nose, almost distracting him from the question he needed to ask even if he didn't want to. "How much have you read? Do you know…"

"No. I've worked out what Malcolm and Matthew were doing but I'm not up to where you were born yet."

He breathed a sigh of relief. It would be short lived though; as much as he didn't want to know the answer to his parentage, he needed to.

In spite of Ren's protests, without that knowledge he couldn't move forward.

Not if he wanted them to have a worry-free future. With the secret hanging over his head, he'd always be waiting for it to come out. For her to realize his origins were something she couldn't live with.

"Stop it." She slapped his bare ass.

"Hey!"

"Nothing that is in those books can change this. *Us.*"

"How can you be so sure?" he demanded, a harsh edge to his voice.

"Because I loved you in spite of the fact I hated you."

18

BECAUSE I LOVED you in spite of the fact I hated you.

Ren's words had been on repeat in his head for the last two days. And he still couldn't wrap his mind around them. Brady wasn't sure he ever would. All he could do was accept them.

"Stop going over it."

He turned his head for a second before refocusing on the snow-slick mountain road in front of them. "What?"

Her hand landed on his thigh. "You know what. If you leaving and not contacting me for thirteen years didn't affect it, nothing I find in your mother's books will change the way I feel."

"You don't know that."

"Actually, I do." Her fingers tightened on his leg momentarily. "You want me to trust you, Brady, but that goes both ways. You need to trust that what I say is the truth. That when I tell you I love you, I mean it, and when I say nothing can change that, you have to *believe* it."

He sighed. "I'm sorry. It's just…"

She squeezed his leg again. "I know. It's okay. We'll get through this and everything will be fine."

God, he wanted to believe that. With every breath he took he wanted to believe she'd stick by his side when all the rotting bones were uncovered because Brady was pretty sure those bones held decaying flesh—rotting, festering maggot-filled flesh.

"It's not far now, just around the next bend. Steve's place has a big driveway so if we're the last to arrive you can still pull in off the road," Ren instructed.

"Are we late?" The last thing he wanted was to be late when he'd asked to meet with everyone.

"No. No. Gordie invited everyone over for dinner. She promised to keep the true reason for getting together a secret until you were ready."

"*We*, until *we* were ready. This is about us now. I know it's my family, my past, but if we're mates that makes it your family, your past."

"Okay, then I'm ready whenever you are."

Brady could hear Ren's determination to stand by his side, her confidence that the people inside Steve and Gordie's house wouldn't run him out of town, and it had his spine straightening, his shoulders pulling back. Drawing in a deep breath, he let the anxiety rolling in his gut out as he exhaled.

"I think we should dive right in. No point dragging this out longer than we have to," he said. "It's not like putting it off gets us anything, and I'm ready to move on, to let all the secrets out so they're no longer hanging over my head."

"Our heads. It's hanging over *our* heads. And I agree. We get it done so we can move past it. I'll let Gordie know as soon as we get there."

He nodded, kept his gaze on the road, and sent up a silent wish that revealing what they'd discovered didn't mean he'd be finding a new place to live, that he'd be forced to take Ren away or worse, give her up.

Ren slapped his thigh. "Stop it! You're not going anywhere. *I'm* not going anywhere."

"What? Are you reading my mind now?"

"No, but I'm sensing your agitation; it's like the air thickened or something." She twisted in her seat, both hands now on his leg, her grip firm. "I get why you're worried but nothing we've uncovered was your doing. I know these people. They aren't about to blame you for something you never had a hand in."

Glancing quickly at Ren, he offered a small smile, before looking forward again. "I'll keep you to those words."

"You can. I promised I'd never lie to you and I won't, not even now when a lie might make you feel better."

Brady could hear the truth in her voice. She wouldn't lie. Not about this. She'd told him some of what she'd read in his mother's journals; he knew she hadn't found out if Michelle Watson was his birth mother yet. God. Michelle hadn't even been married to Malcolm Connelly. She'd been kidnapped and held captive until she'd lost the will—the desire—to escape.

Ren hadn't revealed the details of Michelle's early life in Whispering Springs although she'd given him enough to know the young woman his mother had been was subjected to isolation and brutal abuse. If Brady had to guess, he'd say at some point her kidnapper had become her savior.

Brady wasn't sure if he wanted to know all the details or keep his knowledge to a more general overview. What he did know was that they had to find out what Malcolm and this Matthew person had been doing with the children they brought to the mountains over the years.

"Here. Turn in here."

He took his foot off the accelerator and lightly touched the brake. The last thing he needed to do was put them in a ditch because he'd slammed on the brakes like some rookie driving in the snow for the first time.

Comfortable with his speed, Brady made the turn into the driveway of a huge log cabin. Only the house in front of them couldn't really be called a cabin. More like a mansion.

"Steve built this?" he asked as he brought the truck to a stop beside a sheriff's department SUV.

"I know, right?" Ren leaned forward in her seat, her gaze roaming over the beautiful house. "I knew Steve was good with his hands, a regular handyman around town, but I had no idea he was this good until he and Gordie got together and I came up here."

"I might have to talk to him about our place."

"He's good at the design aspect of a house too. According to Gordie, he designed and built this place himself with a little labor help here and there. Wait until you see the hand carved furnishings. I love the railing he did for the stairs leading to the bottom level."

"Are those the ones Gordie fell down?"

Between reading his mother's journals, Ren had told him what had happened in recent months, including her sister's accident at the beginning of the year. Brady was astonished to discover Gordie had walked away from her encounter with Marcus virtually unscratched but a tumble down a flight of stairs left her with a busted arm and an almost busted head.

Humming agreement, Ren tipped her chin up and said, "We've been spotted."

Brady's gaze zipped to the front door. Sure enough, two people stood in the open doorway. Gordie and Steve. "I met

Gordie the other day so she's easy to place but I can't believe how recognizable Steve is. He hasn't changed at all."

"I know, I swear that man doesn't age. He looks the same as he did in high school."

"What, no wrinkles or gray hairs?" he asked with a smile.

"Not that I've seen. Although my sister would be to blame for those, not the years he's added to his life."

"Well, let's get this over with." Brady switched off the truck and unlatched his seatbelt. "No point delaying the inevitable."

Ren laughed as she undid her belt and opened her door. "You sound like you're going to the gallows."

"Feels like I might be," he muttered as he popped open his door. Brady barely had his feet on the ground and the door closed behind him when Ren threw herself at him. He had no choice but to catch her. "Hey!"

"Please stop it," she mumbled into his neck where she'd tucked her face after wrapping her arms and legs around him in a death-grip. "Everything is going to be fine."

Brady sighed. "I know. I just don't like being the bearer of bad news. Or the one whose family tried to destroy this town and the pack. And I don't want to even think about what Marcus tried to do to Gordie."

"I wouldn't either but I know nobody would blame me for what others did." She leaned back until their gazes locked. "No one will hold you responsible for Marcus's or Malcolm's actions. And if they do, they'll have to deal with me."

He grinned at the fierce look on Ren's face, the murderous glint in her eyes. His one-woman army defending him from the world.

Sliding a hand to the back of her head, he held her gaze with his as surely as he held her head. "Thank you. Thank you for defending me, for standing up for me when I'm not sure I should stand up for myself."

"You have nothing to defend against. You were a powerless kid before and then you weren't here. Nothing that happened while you were away can be laid at your feet and anything we discover in your mother's books isn't on you either. You haven't even read them. Only your mother and I know what's written on those pages."

Ren was right, his brain knew she was; it was just his heart, the one that ached to be accepted in the Whispering Mountains pack once more, felt heavy, like this could be the thing that turned the pack members against him.

She rested her forehead on his, her arms tightening around his neck. "We've got this."

Her words were a vow. Filled with strength and conviction and trust. Trust in *them*. Trust in *him*. "I love you."

Grinning, she smacked her mouth on his then jumped out of his arms, grabbed his hand, and tugged him toward the house. "Ditto. Now let's get this done."

With a smile, Brady let her pull him in spite of the fact he'd willingly follow her anywhere. They'd come a long way in such a short time. Only a few days and he'd lay his life down for hers. He had no doubt she'd do the same. And in that moment he realized she was right.

He had nothing to worry about from the members of the Whispering Mountains pack because all that really mattered was the woman with her hand in his. The woman who loved him no matter what had happened in the past.

Ren.

"Hey." He pulled her to a stop.

Looking over her shoulder, she arched an eyebrow.

"Why don't you go by Ren anymore?" He had wanted to know since old Doc Monroe had told him she'd stopped using it after he'd left.

With a sigh, she turned to face him. "You want to do this now?"

Brady nodded.

"Okay." She licked her lips, swallowed, then licked them again. "If I wasn't allowed to say your name or ask about you, I couldn't live with the reminder of you. You made me Ren and without you I couldn't bear to hold onto her."

Fuck. He closed his eyes, held her hand tighter.

She killed him. Slashed his heart wide open.

His fucking father had done that and Brady hadn't been here to protect her. With a quick tug, he yanked her into him and wrapped his arms around her.

Opening his eyes, he locked his gaze on hers. "You can't imagine how much it hurts me to know I didn't—couldn't—protect you from Malcolm or Marcus. But what hurts the most is that you felt as though you couldn't be Ren without me. You didn't, don't, need me to be her."

She shrugged. "It felt that way at the time."

"I'll never call you Kat." He grinned. "Seems a little weird to call a canine shifter Kat but that's not why I won't do it."

Brady palmed her face and brought his lips to hers. He didn't take the kiss deep, only pressed his lips to hers and absorbed the pleasure being able to do so gave him.

"I love you. I've always loved you, will always love you. No matter what you called yourself while I was gone, you are and always have been Ren. It's not my love or me that makes you her, it's who you are, and who you are makes me love you."

Ren rolled her lips inward, her eyes sparkling with moisture. "Brady," she breathed against his mouth.

He shook his head. "That didn't sound right. I mean—" She placed her fingers over his lips.

"No. It came out perfectly because it wasn't perfect. I know what you meant and I have to say it's the most wonderful thing anyone has ever said to me."

"Really?" Brady asked, skeptical that no one else had told her how important she was to them. "Your parents and sister have never said they love you?"

Smiling, Ren trailed her fingers along his jaw. "It's not the words of love that make what you said perfect, Brady; it's the reason you love me."

"The reason? Because you're you?" Now he was really confused. Didn't they love her for her?

She leaned in and brushed her mouth on his. "C'mon. Let's leave this particular talk for later and go have a different one."

Brady glanced over her shoulder toward the house where Gordie and Steve waited. He'd forgotten where they were, why they were here. "I'd prefer to keep this conversation going," he muttered.

"Me too." Ren laughed. "But considering I'd like to jump your bones right now and I don't think my sister would appreciate me doing that on her front lawn, we should really go have that other talk."

His gaze now back on Ren, a growl rumbling in his chest, he palmed her ass and lifted her against him so she could feel one bone in particular. "Do not tell me you want to jump my bones when I have to spend the next few hours with your family and friends."

"That bone. That's the one I want to jump."

Before Brady could drag her back to the truck and drive away, Ren pulled from his grip and ran for the door.

"Ren," he called as he took off after her.

Laughing she yelled, "Catch me if you can," and darted around her sister and into the house.

Faced with a smiling Steve and Gordie, he wasn't sure what

to say or do. He was thankful for the longish sweater he wore though. At least they wouldn't be able to see the evidence of his lust.

Then again, coyote shifters, so they probably heard every word they'd spoken and could smell both his and Ren's arousal.

Ignore and distract. Brady held out his hand. "Hi, Gordie, nice to see you again."

Gordie eyed his offering then laughed. "I think we're beyond that, don't you?"

Confused, Brady almost didn't return the hug Gordie laid on him. "Oh. Right." When she let him go, Brady found Steve waiting with his hand out.

"I think we'll stick with handshakes," Steve said.

"Good. Yes. Handshakes." Brady slid his hand into Steve's.

"Welcome to the family," Steve added as they shook.

Caught off guard again, Brady glanced between the two of them. "Family?"

Gordie smiled and patted his cheek. "Yes. Welcome. Mom and Dad are going to be thrilled."

"Ah..."

Steve laughed and pulled him into the house.

Brady hadn't even realized he hadn't let go of the other man's hand. Rectifying that quickly, he glanced around and instantly found something to say.

"This place is amazing. Ren said you designed and built it yourself?" he asked as he turned to face Steve.

Steve gave him a smile that said he knew exactly what Brady was doing by bringing up the house. "Yes. I'll give you the grand tour—"

"We should get back to everyone first," Gordie interrupted.

Taking a deep breath, Brady nodded. "Yes. We should get the unpleasantness out of the way."

Steve motioned for Gordie to go first. "By all means, let's get this over with. Or started depending on your point of view."

Brady looked between his hosts; he wasn't sure because he hadn't seen either in years but he'd swear by the expressions on their faces he wasn't the only one going into this meeting with something hanging over his head.

19

KAT TOOK A SEAT BESIDE BRADY. She hadn't had to
tell Gordie to get straight to the reason they were here; apparently Brady had done that when he'd followed her inside after
she'd teased him.

She probably shouldn't have done that, but she'd wanted
him to think about something other than what they were about
to reveal for just a few moments.

Her plan had worked. A little too well really, because now
she was aroused and everyone in the room knew it. Damn
stupid coyote senses. At least they didn't have to worry about
announcing their recent mating bond.

Their mutual marks might be hidden by their clothes but
for a room full of coyote shifters, seeing those bite marks
wouldn't be necessary. Within seconds of them entering the
house, their mated status would have been obvious.

They'd made quick work of the introductions and with
Brady having grown up here, he didn't require in-depth details.
Now that everyone had taken a seat, the room filled with
tension, the air vibrating with anticipation.

Kat wanted to believe no one was looking at Brady as a threat but she couldn't deny that with the last name Connelly, his presence put everyone on edge.

She wasn't sure if Gordie or Steve had told anyone the real reason why they were here, not that it mattered. They'd all know soon enough.

"I know you all came here expecting a nice dinner with friends and to welcome our newest pack member, and we will get to that, I promise." Gordie smiled at her and Brady as she spoke. "Brady and my sister have some things to say, but *I* need to tell you all what I've discovered first, and while it's not the reason for this meeting, I feel it has something to do with what Brady and Kat are going to share."

"Just spit it out, Doc." Steve put an arm around his wife. "They're not going to shoot the messenger."

"I ran some tests. Before Brady came to town. I didn't know there was anyone to claim the bodies and I wanted to add to my research—"

"Doc, get to the point," Steve urged.

Kat glanced around the room; no one appeared to have a clue what Gordie was talking about but Kat's gut told her it wasn't going to be a surprise to her. Or Brady.

"It's okay, Gordie." Kat took Brady's hand in hers and gave it a reassuring squeeze. "Whatever you have to say isn't going to be worse than what we've discovered." She deliberately used "we" so everyone knew she stood beside Brady in this.

"Oh." Gordie sighed. "Okay. Well, anyway, as I said, I ran some tests. You all know I'm researching the coyote gene and whether it strengthens or weakens when mixed with human DNA. I acquired Malcolm's DNA when he was killed in his attempt to run Quinn over. It's how I determined the origin of the turned shifters who had shown up during that time period. That they were turned by Malcolm Connelly."

"The council blamed Malcolm for those and numerous other incidents, but I'm not sure some of it shouldn't fall on the younger Connelly's shoulders," Quinn said.

"It shouldn't. The shifters I mean. It was definitely Malcolm who turned the humans. It couldn't have been Marcus." Gordie looked at Brady, her hands twisting in front of her and Kat knew what she was going to say before she said it. "Marcus wasn't a Connelly by blood. My tests show he was a non-blood. And I don't have a record of the DNA line that he was turned by."

"What the fuck?" Brogan surged to his feet. "How the hell was Marcus non-blood? Connelly was full-blood; his son had to be at least half-blood."

"Malcolm brought Marcus to the mountains as a two-year-old and gave him to my mother." Brady said, drawing every eye in the room.

Kat held her breath. She'd let him lead this; she might be the one with the knowledge, the one who'd read Michelle's journals, but it was Brady's information to share.

"What did you say?" Dale asked, rising slowly to his feet. "Your father *gave* Marcus to your mother?"

"Ren and I have been going through my mother's things." Brady snorted. "That's if she even is my mother. She definitely wasn't Marcus's. At this point we don't know all the details. We're only partway through the journals she left. Ren has been taking notes. I don't think we should reveal everything we've discovered until we've finished reading all the entries and have a clearer view of what happened."

Dale strode forward, moving beside Brogan who stood in front of Brady, the sheriff's glower as fierce as the sovereign's. "I'm sure our sovereign agrees with me when I say I think you should explain yourself," he growled as he leaned in.

Kat moved closer to Brady on the couch. She straightened

her spine, sat as tall as she could, and lifting her chin a notch, she raised her voice and commanded, "Sit down. Lording it over us from up there isn't going to get you answers."

"Ren. It's okay," Brady murmured, squeezing her hand. "I'm sure—"

"No, it's not okay. None of this is your fault, and we're in a position to explain what, until now, has been the unexplainable. If they don't play nice, neither will we." Kat tipped her chin up further and crossed her arms, her eyes daring either man to argue with her. "You want your answers, you sit down and listen, and only listen. You can ask questions after we finish telling you what we've discovered so far."

"Fair enough. But I want access to those journals," Brogan said taking his seat once more.

Dale took a moment to stare Brady down before glancing her way then following their sovereign's lead. The sheriff's gaze told Kat he wanted to make it clear while they weren't enemies, as sheriff he wouldn't let them get away with not answering.

"Kat is right. No one is going to blame you for anything your parents may have done, Brady."

Kat was glad for the sheriff's concession even if it sounded forced.

Ignoring Dale's words, Brady turned and addressed Gordie. "I'd like to come into the clinic and have you run tests on my blood. I think you'll find I'm not a Connelly either."

"Jesus. And the crazy just keeps on crazying," Quinn said, with a sigh. "I think you better explain why you think that."

"We've barely started with the journals. My mother seems to have written the majority of them after leaving the mountain. I don't know exactly what they cover. We know Marcus was brought here as a child and my mother was told to raise him."

"They're labeled by year and some have a name inside the

front cover, but I think they might overlap timewise a bit too," Kat added. "Which is why I've been taking my own notes."

"According to the journals, Marcus was turned at the age of four by old man Baker." Brady revealed the one piece of information Gordie didn't seem to have.

Brady's words had Dale straightening in his chair, his hands clenching, his breath sucking in hard.

Tatum stiffened beside him. "Cade," she whispered, her hand finding one of Dale's.

Kat focused on Tatum, and whispered, "There's a book with the name Cade inside it. I haven't read it yet because I tried to put them into order before I started."

"Oh god." Tatum wrapped her arms around her expanded belly and bent forward. Dale reached over and scooping her up, placed her in his lap and cuddled her close.

"What year?" Dale ground out through clenched teeth.

"From what I've worked out, he would have been six," Kat offered in a louder voice.

Tatum buried her face in the side of Dale's neck and he held her tight, buried his nose in her hair, and whispered nonsense words Kat couldn't hear.

It took him a moment to get his emotions under control. When he did, Dale turned to Brogan. "I want that book."

Brogan nodded. "Once Brady and Kat have gone over everything, we'll make sure you get that one."

"How many other names are there?" Gordie asked, her gaze a mix of shock and curiosity. Kat could almost hear her sister's brain whirring around with possibilities.

Kat looked to Brady, tried to telegraph with her eyes it was up to him if he wanted to reveal that information now. He gave her a nod.

"Including Cade I found ten names written inside the covers."

"I don't recognize any of the names other than Cade. Those of you who are older and never left Whispering Springs may know them," Brady said. "I'd like this to remain between us until we know exactly what my mother's words reveal."

Brogan leaned forward in his chair, his arms resting on his knees. "Agreed. And if either of you want help going through the journals, let us know."

"Thank you, sovereign. I appreciate that but I'd prefer to know what else is in them before I share with you or anyone else."

"The offer stands." Brogan smiled grimly. "I thank you for your willingness to share this information. It can't be easy for you and I want to reiterate what Dale said earlier. No one will blame you for what Marcus, Malcolm, or Michelle Connelly did."

Brady tipped his chin in acknowledgement.

"Watson," Kat said. "Michelle Watson. She never married Malcolm."

Brady's gaze zipped to hers, his hand landing on her leg in a hard thump. "*Ren.*"

Too late she realized she'd revealed something she shouldn't have. They should have talked before coming here to be sure she knew what she could and couldn't say. "I'm sorry. I didn't mean—"

"It's okay. We should probably tell them that part anyway," Brady said with a sigh. Turning back to the room, he continued. "Michelle Watson was taken from a street in Omaha, Nebraska, and brought to Whispering Springs by Malcolm."

"Taken," Rowan gasped. It was the first time she'd spoken. "He *kidnapped* her? Kept her here all that time? But why didn't she—"

"Stockholm Syndrome," Gordie interrupted. "He had her long enough and isolated enough for it to develop. She didn't start working for Dad until a couple of years after Kat was born. Jesus, Kat would have been around four. She came in with burns to her hands and Dad offered her a job before he'd finished seeing to her wounds."

"Burns?" Brady asked.

"Yes. I remember because it was the first time Dad let me into an exam room while he worked on a patient. Well, he didn't exactly *let* me in. He was too busy seeing to your mom while our mom took care of you and Marcus."

"And he offered her a job?" Brady shook his head. "I don't remember her not working at the clinic. As far as I knew she worked there every day until..."

Kat stood. "I need to read the rest of those books. Maybe she tried to escape—"

"Ren." Brady stood and grabbed her hands. "They can wait. We'll get the answers and probably a whole bunch more questions we'll never find the answers to, but it can wait."

"But, Brady—"

He yanked her into his chest. Pressed her face into his neck. "No. Let's take the rest of today. Spend some time with your sister and Steve. I know you missed seeing everyone the last few days while we were snowed in."

She smiled. Brady was right. She'd been pacing the floors with a journal in her hand, a notebook beneath it ready for her to jot anything significant down, for days now.

Claustrophobia had never been an issue for Kat but idleness had. Standing still, doing nothing, had never been her thing. She couldn't even stay still long enough to soak in a bath.

The only time she remained in one place was when she was in a kitchen. Except her mind and hands were so busy there she didn't notice the lack of movement.

"We've got plenty of time to read what my mother wrote."

He squeezed her tighter. "Plenty of time to discover if she was my mother at all."

Shit. She'd forgotten to tell him. She was pages away from confirming that Michelle Watson was Brady's mother. In the journal Kat was currently reading, Michelle was pregnant. The joy in the woman could be felt in her words; she'd never made it this far into a pregnancy before and Kat couldn't deny the other woman's happiness had soaked into her words, into the pages of the book.

If she had the timeline right, Michelle was pregnant with Brady and he definitely wasn't a Connelly.

He was Matthew's son.

And she still didn't know who Matthew was or where he'd gone.

Before she had to bit her tongue to stop herself from revealing what she'd read this morning, her brother-in-law saved her.

"Okay, who's hungry?" Steve asked. "Thanks to the Den, we've got a feast waiting to be devoured."

Kat turned to her sister. "You got food from the Den?"

Gordie laughed. "You didn't expect me to cook, did you?"

Kat shook her head. "Jeez, no, but you could have asked me to bring food over."

Linking her arm through Kat's, Gordie tugged her away from Brady. "You did. Wendy sent the last of the beef stew you made before the storm and El brought along a batch of her grandmother's famous spaghetti sauce too."

"I brought bread," Tatum added as they made their way toward the kitchen.

"My contribution is clean up," Rowan added from behind them.

Glancing back, Kat found the men remained in the living

room eyeing the newbie in their midst. She hoped they weren't too rough on Brady.

As if she could read her mind, Gordie said, "Don't worry. They're just going to grill him on his intentions toward you."

Kat laughed. "Only you would think telling me not to worry and then telling me what's about to happen means I won't."

"I think Brady's intentions are clear and I approve, but you know men, they have to thump their chests and grunt a few times before they give their approval," Rowan said as she moved past them with an armload of plates. "I'll get the table set."

"You approve?"

"I most certainly do. And I know what it's like to spend years away from your mate so I'm not about to judge you or him for giving off enough pheromones to slay a bull."

"Oh, but we weren't mates when—"

"Of course you were." Gordie patted Kat's arm. "You were just too young to know it but everyone else did."

"*What?*"

"Well, everyone who took the time to look." Gordie waved a hand in the air. "It doesn't matter. Water under the bridge. Now let's get the food on the table before it goes cold again."

Kat studied her sister. Had Gordie known Brady was Kat's mate all those years ago? She hadn't but Gordie was older by six years; she would have known what was building between her and Brady because she would have seen it in others. She'd also been close to Rowan before the accident, would have known about and understood the bond between their friend and Quinn.

Jeez. Kat closed her eyes and sucked in a breath. Why hadn't she been able to work out why Brady's disappearance had hurt so badly?

Hindsight. It was a brilliant thing. She hadn't only been in love with Brady all those years ago, she'd stayed in love with him. Through no contact and a furious hatred that was spawned by the actions of his father and brother—who weren't related to him at all.

She had to tell him what she'd read this morning; whether she knew for sure or not, he needed to know what she suspected.

And they needed to find out who Matthew was.

20

BRADY STARED AT REN. Surely he hadn't heard what he thought... "Say that again."

"Michelle is your mother. You're her biological child."

"And my father?" Every muscle in his body locked up.

"Matthew."

"Who the fuck is Matthew?"

"He's the man I asked you about before. The one who lived here. Are you sure you don't remember him?" Ren asked.

Shaking his head, Brady paced the living room. "No. I barely remember my—Malcolm—being here. I tried to stay out of his way, stuck close to Mom, or hid in my room." He dragged a hand down his face. "Are you sure she's my real mother?"

Ren confirmed with a simple nod.

God, he'd hoped. Prayed. And the relief rushing through him told him just how much he'd *needed* to be Michelle Watson's child. Anything else he could deal with, but obviously that would have been his breaking point. "Okay," he breathed out. "Okay."

"I want to skim through the rest of the journals, see if I can find out who Matthew is and where we might find him now."

"Find him?" Brady shook his head. "No. Absolutely not. He's mentioned in the journals up until now. There's no way he didn't know what Malcolm had done—was doing—to Michelle. I don't want to find him. I want to kill him."

"But—"

He held up a hand. "No."

Before Ren could argue further, he left the room. The walls were closing in on him. His skin felt too tight. His bones itchy.

Knowing exactly what he needed, he headed for the back door, stripping along the way. Naked, he grabbed the handle and yanked the door open. Brady let the shift take him and bounded out of the house into the snow-covered yard.

His thought processes worked the same in coyote form except he always found they flowed more easily when he worked his canine body into a sweat. Doing it in human form never had quite the same result.

He ran between the trees, dodged around drifts of snow. Within a few minutes, his heart pumped as fast as his paws, and his mind worked in rhythmical circles until he felt calm enough to return to human form.

Return to Ren.

She waited for him on the back porch, his clothes clutched to her chest. "Better?" she asked as he crossed the yard toward her, his pace far slower than it had been moments ago.

From one step to the next, he changed to his human body, a smile curling his lips. "Yes. Sorry. I seem to run out on you a lot."

With a shrug she held out his jeans. "It's what clears your head. I cook. You run."

Smiling wider, Brady stepped one leg into his pants. "I seem to run more than you cook."

"I don't have as much weighing on my mind as you do right now."

Brady stopped with his jeans halfway up his thighs and frowned. "Not exactly a prized mate, am I?"

Ren's gaze traveled down his torso until she reached his groin; a smile kicked up one side of her mouth. "Oh, I don't know. You look like a prize to me."

"Oh?" He couldn't stop his body from reacting to her blatant stare of approval and he didn't bother to hide the fact either. Letting go of his pants he stood straight. "See something you want?"

"I see something I have." Her eyes met his once more.

Understanding, compassion, love, lust, so many emotions swirled in the dark brown orbs that Brady felt it like a kick to the gut. "You're not going anywhere, are you?"

Smiling, she shook her head. "Not on threat of death."

"I don't know what I did to deserve this complete devotion from you but I swear, I'll spend every second of my life making sure you don't regret giving it to me."

"All you have to do is give me the same."

"You have that already."

"Then we're good." She held out his shirt. "Want to finish getting dressed or do you want to take those jeans off again and come help me with mine?"

Brady didn't need to think about it. He shucked his pants and kicked them away before stalking toward her. "You want me to help you out here or inside? Because you have about two seconds before I make that decision for you," he growled.

When they returned home from her sister's house, Ren had gone straight to his mother's journals and not lifted her head until a few minutes ago when she had told him Michelle Watson was his biological mother.

He'd found it hard not to drag her off to their room the

second they'd stepped foot in the house but he had done it. She hadn't seemed as wound up as he was or she'd been able to put it aside to focus on his mother's words.

He wasn't so lucky; she'd had him in a slow simmer of lust since the minute he'd entered the Den and after she'd teased him earlier, Brady had spent an uncomfortable few hours surrounded by people and with no hope of getting his mate alone and naked.

Of course once there was hope, Ren had other ideas.

It seemed as though he'd spent most of their recent relationship fighting to get close to her in one way or another.

At least now she was his and when he could get close, there was nothing stopping him from taking her. Claiming her.

"Ren?"

The smile she sent him had his balls tucking up tight. Her next move had his groin throbbing in a painful beat. And the next thing she did seized his lungs. Watching her strip out of her clothes just might kill him. Piece by piece, she discarded each article of clothing without taking her eyes from his.

Naked she stood tall, her shoulders back so her breasts thrust out, tempting him with their taut peaks. "Here."

"You want me to take you out here? In the cold?"

"On the swing." She pointed to the old seat he'd repaired the third day he was here. "I want you on the swing."

Arching an eyebrow he contemplated how best to do this without either of them suffering an injury.

"I'm not sure it will support us..."

And if it didn't, he wanted to be between her and the splintered remains of the chair.

Images flashed through his head, in a second he knew how he wanted to do this.

Striding over, he sat down and patted his thighs. "Climb on."

Ren walked toward him, an exaggerated sway to her hips. "You going to take me for a ride?"

"Think you can handle it?" he asked, knowing it would get her back up a little, which meant he was in for one hell of a ride because she'd be out to prove she could.

"Oh, Brady. Brady, Brady, Brady." She threw a leg over his, giving him a close look at the wet flesh between her legs. "You can't fool me. You know I'm up for it. The question is, are you?"

"I'm up for whatever you want, whenever and wherever you want and if I'm not"—breath hissed through his teeth when she wrapped her hand around his cock—"I'll die in my effort to keep up."

"No one's dying here. Unless we're talking about what the French refer to as the little death." Eyes on his, she rose, maneuvered his shaft into place, and held it tight. "Are you ready for a *little death*, Brady?"

"I'm ready for anything—everything—with you." Grabbing her hips, he lifted his own and drove his length deep then paused. "Only you."

Cupping one side of his face, Ren leaned in and brushed her lips on his. "Only you."

With a grin, Brady bucked his hips and said, "Let's ride off into the sunset together."

Ren groaned, rolled her eyes. "Jeez. Corny much?"

"You love me," he answered and rocked into her once more.

"Yeah, I do."

"Then marry me." It wasn't really a question and he accompanied the words with a tweak of her nipples.

"Yes." She moaned, her head falling back before it snapped back up. "Wait. What?"

Brady smiled. "We're doing this so let's do it right. Marry me."

"God. You're insane. We've only just—"

"Ren." He took his hands from her breasts and cradled her face. "I love you. You're my mate. I plan to spend my life with you. I want to do it with my ring on your finger and yes, we've moved fast but we know. We *know*."

Her eyes bounced between his, emotions tangling and tumbling in quick succession, and he saw it the moment she got it, got him. "Yes. Okay, yes, let's get married," she said with a laugh.

"There's my Ren." He loved seeing her sparkle with joy, and he hadn't realized until now he hadn't seen it this pure since before he left. Right then he vowed to make sure every day she felt this happy, smiled this brightly. "I missed you. Fuck, did I miss you."

Smiling, her eyes watery, she leaned in and pressed her mouth to his. "I missed you too. Don't leave me again, Brady."

"Never," he promised.

"Good." She rolled her hips. "Now, let's take that ride into the sunset."

21

JANUARY 29

BRADY TOOK a deep breath and addressed the four men in the room. "Thank you for coming out here. Ren and I are ready to tell you what my mother's journals reveal. Then if you wouldn't mind, I'd like all of you to accompany me when I open the shed out back."

He'd given Dale a rundown of what opening the shed was about, and he was glad to see the sheriff had arrived in uniform with a full kit for evidence collection. The other men were also here in their official capacities. Brogan Wilder, the pack sovereign, his regal Quinn MacClellan, and head councilman William Brant.

With a nod to Ren, Brady leaned back in his seat and let her take over.

"Like Brady said, thank you for coming and for your discretion. When I'm done explaining what we've learned, I'll hand everything over for you to go through and do with as you see fit."

"You don't want to keep the journals?" Brogan asked.

"Not particularly. I won't ever read them and I'm pretty sure Ren isn't interested in a re-read." They'd talked about it, he and Ren, and while it was his history, the history of his mother, Brady preferred to hold on to the good memories and keepsakes.

Plus he was pretty sure the sheriff's department would want to take them in as evidence along with whatever was left behind in the shed after all these years.

"Okay, then. When you're ready," Dale addressed Ren.

"I'll do this in point form, a timeline of sorts, and then you can ask questions or go over any of the books. I've labeled them by year and major event."

After receiving nods from everyone, Ren continued.

"Michelle Watson was snatched off a street in Omaha, Nebraska, and brought here. She was held captive, beaten, and sexually assaulted for a number of years before Malcolm allowed her to interact with other pack members. During those years Malcolm Connelly and a man known only as Matthew—"

"Caldwell. Matthew Caldwell. He lived with the Connellys from the time he was a child until he up and left without a word," William Brant explained. "Malcolm was always vague about where he'd gone and why."

"We'll get to where he went in a bit," Ren offered. "As I was saying, during those years, Malcolm and Matthew would take trips to the city and kidnap toddlers. From what Michelle knew, Malcolm would receive a call, leave here, and return with a child who they would keep in the shed out back for no more than a week before they took the child away never to be seen again."

"Except Marcus." Quinn interrupted. "Brady, you said Malcolm gave him to your mother."

"He did. From what my mother wrote, Marcus was the first child they brought here but we can't know that for sure. He might just be the first she knew about. We've compiled a list of names and other than Cade Flint, none of them are familiar," Brady answered. "And everything about Cade is different from the others. He was older and he remained here in Whispering Springs."

"In my opinion that happened because he was older. They couldn't convince him he wasn't Cade Flint in the days they held him in the shed," Ren added.

"Fuck." Dale shoved his fingers through his hair. "He never said a word."

"I think I know why." Ren's gaze connected with Brady's and he nodded. "Cade was given to the Bakers, and four years after he was brought to Whispering Springs, he returned to the Connelly property and the shed he was held in where he found Matthew and a newborn boy. According to Michelle's journal entry, Cade set fire to the shed with Matthew and the baby inside."

"Michelle managed to get the baby out but Matthew died when the roof collapsed on him. Malcolm buried his body beneath the shed before erecting a new one. We believe the body is still there," Brady added.

"That explains your request for me to be here in an official capacity," Dale muttered. "But I'm not sure I should be the one to oversee this with my connection to Cade."

"I don't think you'll compromise evidence or disregard it due to Cade's involvement. I have no objections to you taking lead on this. Anyone else?" Brogan asked.

"Sovereign is right, you're more likely to seek the truth due to Cade's involvement and at this point it's not as though he could be charged," William added.

"There isn't much information other than first names and dates on the children, but we do have something else significant that you might be interested in. The reason Michelle finally escaped Malcolm and left the mountain. The day she fled, she'd broken her silence and told Maggie Wilder about everything."

"Goddamn motherfucker." Brogan surged to his feet and pointed at William. "He killed them. I knew it wasn't an accident and you wouldn't do anything about it."

"I couldn't do anything even if the evidence that was presented suggested foul play," William argued. "Which it didn't."

Turning to Dale, Brogan commanded, "Reopen the case into my parents' deaths."

"Sovereign." Dale nodded.

Brady knew they needed to get to the final part of why they were here. Clearing his throat, he brought everyone's attention back to him and said, "The newborn caught in the shed with Matthew was registered as the child of Michelle, father unknown, but my mother's journals reveal the child was my full brother. Matthew fathered myself and the infant named Jacob. Both of us were given the last name Connelly because Malcolm didn't know Matthew and Michelle were sleeping together."

"What happened to the baby?" William asked.

"Michelle's journal entry for that day says after she'd gone to town to have the burns she received trying to rescue the baby and Matthew treated, she returned home and found the baby and Malcolm gone. When he returned—without Jacob— Malcolm handed her paperwork. A birth certificate and adoption papers. He'd forged her signature and given the baby away." Ren flipped through her notepad. "It's at this point that Malcolm began to show signs of mental instability. Michelle writes on a number of occasions that his moods become more and more volatile and his drinking increased."

"I tried a number of times to have him removed as sovereign due to his alcoholism," William added. "It wasn't until it got out of hand and he was drunk all day every day that the council started to realize he was no longer a good fit for the role. Of course it still took him attacking Brogan and challenging him to a fight for the position before they made any moves against him."

"Not that they needed to do anything when Malcolm disappeared over the ridge," Quinn growled.

"Anything else we need to discuss before we move outside? I'd like to start before the light fades," Dale explained as he stood, changing the direction of the discussion.

"Tell us what to do and we'll do it," Brogan said. "Anything your deputies would normally do."

"How are you with a shovel?" Dale asked, grinning.

Quinn flexed his arms. "All that snow shoveling is finally paying off."

Laughing, William pushed to his feet. "If it's okay with you youngsters, I'll sit the shoveling out."

"You can be in charge of the log," Dale said, handing the councilman a notepad and pen. "Write down everything we do. Also, I'll get you to label the evidence bags. Kat? Can you take pictures of the whole process?"

"Sure. Should I start before or after you cut the locks off?"

"Before. I want everything documented."

"Right, everyone has their jobs; let's get this done." Brogan headed toward the door where he picked up one of the shovels Brady had place there earlier in preparation.

He was relieved to have the subject of Malcolm Connelly

out of the spotlight. Now they could concentrate on his father. Brady had been glad to discover he wasn't Malcolm's biological child except the unknown Matthew didn't appear to be a better option.

Both men had done horrible things according to his mother, and Brady hadn't come to terms with who his father was or his mother's apparent love for the man. And she had loved him. In some twisted way, Matthew had become Michelle's savior, the reason she hadn't tried to escape before the night Malcolm had gone on a murderous rampage.

Why Michelle hadn't left after Matthew's death still wasn't clear, but Ren had her theory on that. She thought Michelle had stayed in the hope of Malcolm revealing where he'd taken her youngest son. Whether Malcolm had worked out who'd fathered Jacob remained unknown but to Brady's mind it was clear. Malcolm had known.

It wouldn't surprise Brady to discover Malcolm had known he wasn't his child either.

"Hey." Ren slipped her arm through his. "You okay?"

"Hmm." Glancing down he offered a smile. "Yeah, I'm good. I'll be better when this is over, but now that we know everything we're going to from my mother's journals, we can move forward."

"You still happy to leave Jacob—"

"For now. Let's deal with the shed. Get married next week and enjoy some quiet before we rock the boat again."

"You're sure?"

God, he loved her. He'd made the mistake of telling her he didn't want to upset their wedding plans by looking for Jacob. Now she thought he was putting it off for her when really, he was doing it for himself. He needed to wrap his head around the fact he had another brother. One that was actually blood related. "It's been twenty-two years. A few more weeks won't make a difference."

"But—"

"Ren. I'm not ready."

"Oh. Okay." She frowned, studied him intently, her concern clear.

"I'm good, Ren. Honestly."

"Hey, you two, are we doing this or not?" Dale asked, half out the door.

"We should get this done. I want to sleep with you in my arms tonight, knowing there isn't a body buried in the backyard." Brady urged her after Dale.

"It's not exactly in the backyard."

"Close enough."

"I can't believe we're actually digging up a skeleton. We've been uncovering proverbial ones for days and now we're looking for a real one."

"Did you tell Gordie she could have whatever we find after the sheriff is done with it?" he asked, picking up the last shovel. He wouldn't ask his pack mates to do anything he wouldn't do, and that included digging up bodies.

"Yes. She wanted to be here but I convinced her it would be best to waited until Dale called. Once you find what we're after, he'll call her in to transport the body—bones, whatever— to town."

And that would be the point where the secret would get out. No way could they hope no one saw them wheeling a body into the clinic. He was ready for that. Had prepared for what he'd say. Until Dale concluded his investigation it would be a clear "no clue, I haven't lived here in years".

Brady figured that line would work for a while and until it didn't, it was all he'd disclose. Of course he'd avoid all conversation if possible.

"C'mon, Dale has the bolt cutters ready." Ren tugged on his hand. "He can't start until I've taken pictures."

He followed Ren and thought about all the changes to his life in the last two weeks.

Fourteen days.

Such a short time in the grand scheme of things and yet...

He'd come home.

Found his mate.

Bonded with his mate.

Discovered his father wasn't his father.

Uncovered a long lost brother.

And now he was digging up the bones of a man he'd never know but would be connected to for eternity.

It seemed to be far too much for fourteen days.

Overwhelming when he listed it all out.

The one bright spot was the woman walking in front of him. She held him up—held him together—just by breathing.

Kathren Joy Monroe was the light of his life and he couldn't wait to marry her next week and become Mr. Kathren Joy Monroe.

They'd spent the last few days talking about his last name. He wasn't a Connelly, and honestly, who would want to keep that or take that as a surname here in Whispering Springs?

Caldwell didn't fit either. So after asking Doc Monroe if he objected, Brady had decided to take Ren's name as his when they made their union legal.

It would remove the last of the dark cloud the Connelly name had put over the town and pack. And Brady wasn't attached to the name at all; in fact it left a bitter taste in his mouth.

Ren's father had suggested he take Hank's surname but that didn't feel as right to Brady as Monroe did.

Over the next few weeks they'd remove everything they

could that tied this place to the past and start laying down new foundations for the future. He had Steve coming over later in the week to draw up plans and Brady hoped to get a start on those before next winter set in.

He wanted this place to become the Monroe place. And for Brady, the day he held Ren's hand and pledged his life to hers, took her name as his, would be the beginning of that. At that point they'd put the past and the Connelly name behind them for good.

EPILOGUE

BRADY LOOKED out over the yard at everyone who had come to help.

They were pulling down the shed. The one that had remained locked until a few weeks ago when the sheriff had broken the locks and gone over every inch of the building looking for evidence.

Not much was left after all these years, but the one thing they did find was Matthew Caldwell's body.

His father.

Jacob's father.

So much had happened in the last month.

Some good, some bad.

"Hey." Ren slid her arm around his waist. "What are you doing standing over here?"

Glancing down, Brady smiled. A whole bundle of good. He wrapped his arm around Ren's shoulders and pulled her in front of him. This right here outweighed all the bad. "I'm just taking one last look before we bury the past for good."

"You know I was thinking..." She looked over her shoulder to where everyone waited. "Do you really want to pull it down? I've got all the makings for s'mores and thought maybe we could burn it to the ground instead. A kind of exorcism, if you like."

"Burn it to the ground?" It was an intriguing idea. It would certainly solve the problem of what to do with all the junk inside. And they could toss on the timber from the old lean-to garage he'd left stacked at the side of the house after he'd ripped it down. "Should we get the fire truck out here?"

Ren patted his chest. "On the way," she said with a grin.

"You planned this?"

"Think of this as our phoenix moment."

"We'll rise from the ashes?"

"Our future."

He caught sight of Brogan and Quinn clearing a perimeter around the shed that had held so much of the bad.

It wasn't the shed Matthew had died in; that one had burned to the ground long ago, but Ren was right.

Exorcism by fire.

Burn away the past and leave the ground fresh for the future. Cleanse this place of all the lies, of all the pain, and allow new life, new memories to take hold.

Memories he'd make with his mate by his side.

BONUS NOVELLA

COYOTE LAW

COYOTE HUNGER BOOK 3.5

For those who kept asking when the next coyote book was coming.
And to Tatum who turned up in Coyote Whispers and showed me who Dale was.

1

DECEMBER 22

DALE FOLLOWED Tatum into Steve's home office and closed the door behind him. "You're not going to make this easy for me, are you?" he asked.

She turned to face him, one eyebrow arched in disbelief. "Should I?"

If he was honest, and he had to be for both their sakes, not to mention the babies she held safe inside her, he didn't deserve for her to make it easy for him. With a large measure of guilt and regret he shook his head. "No. You shouldn't."

Tatum sighed, her shoulders dropping a fraction as her chin lowered to her chest. "I didn't come home to cause you trouble."

"Fuck, Tay, you think I don't know that? You never cause trouble. Always the one smoothing things over, taking care of—"

"I didn't do a good job after Cade." Her gaze met his, her

eyes glassy with unshed tears, and her chin wobbled. "Stupid hormones," she muttered as she used both hands to scrub at her eyes.

"Tay." He didn't know what to do. What to say. He'd gone back for her. To beg her to come to Whispering Springs with him, remind her what they were...

He'd fucked that up when he realized he wasn't as ready as he'd thought. And now she'd turned up here—pregnant.

"Why didn't you tell me?"

"Hard to speak to someone when they sneak out in the middle of the night."

He closed his eyes on a groan. Not his most shining moment, that's for sure. "I'm sorry. So, so sorry. I told you that over a hundred times in voice mails and texts. You never returned one of those messages." The last message he'd left only a few hours ago.

"I could probably accept an apology via phone if it was one time, Dale, but you left me twice. *Twice.*"

"I needed—"

"I don't care what you needed. You. Left. Me." She turned her face away. "I'd already lost Cade..."

Grief tightened his throat, yanked at his chest. "We both lost Cade."

She turned back, anger sparking in her eyes now. "Yes, *we* did. And when *we* should have pulled together, should have leaned on each other, *you* ran."

"I had to get my head on straight. I had to..." He tried to explain but words failed him. He'd been so lost in those first months after Cade. And watching Tatum's grief had only driven him deeper into the darkness choking him.

He'd taken leave from his job and returned to the mountains where he'd spent the early years of his life, more often than not with Cade by his side, and found some peace—hope.

"I'm sorry. I needed to be close to Cade."

"And I didn't?"

"I didn't say that. I just..." He shrugged. God. He was fucking this up. "I wasn't good for you. I couldn't help you if I couldn't help myself."

"So what, you came here, took a new job, and forgot about me!"

"No. Never!" Dale took a step toward her.

She held up a hand. "Don't."

He froze, muscles vibrating with the effort to hold back. He wanted—needed—to hold her, except he'd given up that right. Given up so much when he'd left her behind. He'd never meant for their separation to be permanent but he hadn't told her he was leaving, never mind why or that he'd be back.

Nodding, he murmured, "Okay."

She jerked, her hands going to her swollen belly and rubbing gentle circles. "Dammit. I need to sit down."

"You need to lie down." He risked her anger and moved closer. "Here. Let me help."

Tatum snorted. "Sure. *Now* you want to help."

"I never would have left if I'd known." And if he hadn't been up in his own head which happened to be shoved up his own ass, he would have known they'd finally managed to accomplish their greatest wish. He scooped her into his arms and walked to the couch.

"Jeez, Dale, put me down, I weigh a ton."

"You're light as a feather."

She thumped his chest. "Don't lie to me."

"Fine, you've got about twenty pounds extra on the last time I picked you up." He sank to his knees and lowered her to the couch sideways so she could lie back and stretch her legs out. His gaze was drawn to the mound of her belly. Swallowing hard, he lifted his gaze to hers and asked, "Can I...?"

"What?" she eyed him warily.

"Touch you," he said, tipping his chin toward her stomach.

"You just did. Without asking permission I might add."

"Tay. Please." He couldn't keep the emotions out of his voice, the slight edge of desperation that sliced through him like the deadliest blade.

"Fine." She reached out and grabbed his hand. "Here. Someone's having a hell of time attempting to kick their way out."

She placed his hand low on her right side, just above where her hipbone use to be before her belly grew round with his children. He'd barely made contact when he felt the first thump, a dull punch to his hand as though his palm had been injected with local anesthetic.

God. That was his child in there. Well, one of them anyway. Pressing closer, he cupped this new curve of her body with both hands and waited for more.

Dale had no idea how long they stayed that way, Tatum lying back, eyes closed, letting him feel their child—children— move within her. It wasn't until he heard the delicate snore he hadn't heard in months that he realized she'd fallen asleep. He didn't make a move or sound, just sat on the floor beside her and took her in.

She was beautiful. Even exhausted, with dark shadows beneath her eyes, fatigue etched into the edges of her mouth, she was gorgeous.

He remembered the first time he'd recognized her as his. Cade stood beside him; they'd returned from a run with the pack, when the newly shifted teens came bounding into the clearing. Within seconds everyone shifted to human form and Dale had taken one look at Tatum and lost his breath.

Cade had done the same.

He'd known Cade for as long as he could remember and

sometimes Dale had thought they were one person. They weren't blood related but from the moment they'd met, they were inseparable. Always doing the same things—wanting the same things.

It had never been an issue until Tatum.

They'd been nineteen at the time, Tatum fourteen.

They'd known they were too old for her—that she was too young to be facing a mate, never mind two. Known they had to stay away, but when a coyote found its mate every instinct pushed to claim.

Two years they'd held off.

Two years of watching and waiting and slowly going out of their minds as every eligible boy in Whispering Springs tried to catch the eye of *their* Tatum. They hadn't known it then, but all that worry had been for nothing.

Tatum had set her sights on him and Cade long before her first change.

The death of her father had shaken them all and sent his life in a direction he'd never considered going.

Mrs. Brant—stricken with grief—had packed up and gone back to the city she'd grown up in, taking Tatum and her siblings with her. For Cade and Dale there had been no choice.

They had to follow.

Tatum was barely sixteen and they'd somehow convinced her mother to let them move in with the family—date Tatum. Mrs. Brant's crippling grief helped their cause. She hadn't cared what any of her children did and spent most of her time in her pjs, either in bed or lying on a couch in the living room.

It had fallen to Tatum, Cade, and Dale to see to the raising of Tatum's younger brother and sister.

On Tatum's eighteenth birthday, they'd gone to the local courthouse and acquired the necessary paperwork to make their union—his and Tatum's—legal. Dale couldn't remember how he and Cade had decided which one of them she'd marry. It didn't matter. It didn't change the fact they weren't a couple. They were a trio.

A trio that had fallen apart when a drug dealer—a stupid kid of fifteen—sent three bullets into Cade's chest in a dirty alley.

Dale lowered his head as tears of anger, frustration, guilt, and grief filled his eyes. They'd lost so much more than Cade that night. They'd lost each other. He'd lost himself—his way. He thought he'd finally found it again, but now, with Tatum and the babies...

He couldn't fuck this up. He couldn't lose Tatum and the family they'd always dreamed of.

"We have to work things out, Dale."

Head snapping up, his gaze collided with Tatum's. She reached out a hand and cupped his jaw. Her palm and fingers were soft and cool against his skin, rasping lightly over his stubble.

"Cade would kick both our asses if he was here."

One side of his mouth kicked up. "Yeah, he would."

A yawn big enough to crack her jaw escaped her.

Placing a hand over hers before she could pull it away, he said, "You should get to bed."

Her eyes searched his for long moments. Whatever she saw brought a small smile to her lips. "Okay. We'll leave it for now."

"We're not leaving anything. From now on, you and our babies are my priority."

"How do you know they're yours?" she asked, challenge in her gaze.

"Tay."

"Okay, fine. You've got me. It's not like I can lie about that."

He didn't want to know but he had to ask. "Do you wish they weren't?"

"No!" She pushed herself up, shoved him back with a hand to his shoulder. "Dumbass."

"Name calling?"

"Hey, you've been an ass and now you're being dumb. Ass. Dumb. Dumb—ass." She lifted both hands, palms flat, moving them up and down as though weighing each word as she spoke. Shrugging she added, "If the shoe fits."

Dale held in a smile and nodded. "You're right. I've been a total ass and that was the dumbest question ever asked."

Tatum frown, her eyes narrowing. "That was too easy."

"You haven't seen anything yet. I'm going to be the easiest man you ever met."

"Ah...okay, I have no idea what that means exactly but I'm too tired to work it out now." She swung her legs off the couch and Dale stood, holding out his hand. "I'll go see about that room Steve offered," she added as he pulled her to her feet.

He swallowed around the lump in his throat. "You could—"

Shaking her head, she said, "Don't say it. We're talking after months of not talking and for now that's enough."

"It'll never be enough."

"I'm not the one who walked away, Dale."

He hung his head. *Fuck.* He had so much to make up for. So much he'd missed. "I never intended to stay away," he murmured.

Tatum chuckled and patted her belly. "You didn't stay away."

"That's not what I mean."

"Dale. Please. I'm not mad enough to ignore you. Or keep you out of the babies' lives, but I need time to settle in here. Time to readjust to us living in the same place again." She sighed. "And right now I'm too tired to deal with any of this."

"Sorry." He put a hand on her lower back and urged her

toward the door. "Let's get you settled for the night. We'll worry about everything else tomorrow."

"As long as you don't sneak out in the middle of the night," she muttered.

Dale smiled. "Not a chance."

"Humph."

"You might not believe me," he said as he steered her out of the office and back toward the living room. "But I was coming for you at the end of January."

"Really?" She glanced up, the hope in her eyes almost bringing him to his knees.

"Yeah."

"And by coming for me, you mean moving back to the city?" One eyebrow arched, her brow wrinkled as she glanced at his sheriff's badge.

"No. I was coming to bring you home."

TATUM ROLLED onto her back and blew out a breath.

She'd always slept on her stomach but since her stomach had been invaded by aliens who'd built a second story she'd been forced to find a different position. She'd tried her sides and her back. Even purchased one of those pregnancy body pillows in an attempt to get comfortable.

Ha!

Comfort was a thing of the past. She imagined one baby growing inside you would cause all kinds of discomfort, but two? Yeah, there was no chance she'd get more than a few minutes of sleep at a time. One or the other was always on the move. Or she had to pee. Good thing she'd found it easy to doze off anywhere, anytime. Those cat naps meant she made it through each day without collapsing in complete exhaustion.

"Can't sleep?" Kat's drowsy voice whispered through the dark room they shared.

She'd forgotten how dark nights were in the mountains. "Not since my belly extension."

After a small chuckle Kat was quiet, but Tatum could hear the questions all the same.

She wasn't ready to answer any of them and hoped she wouldn't have to. Not yet.

Not until she'd sorted things out with Dale.

Dale.

Her husband.

The father of her children.

The man who'd walked out when she'd needed him most.

Tatum wasn't sure how they'd find their way back to each other but she knew she wanted to. As much as she wanted to stay angry at Dale, she couldn't stop loving him or walk away.

She'd lost Cade. She'd be damned if she'd lose Dale too.

After Cade's death they'd bumbled their way through a couple of months until she'd woken one morning to find her husband gone. He'd taken nothing with him; his clothes remained in their closet. They were packed now—along with most of her own. On a truck arriving sometime after the first of the year.

In those months before he'd come home, Tatum had known exactly where he was. He'd taken at job in the sheriff's office in their hometown, his pay dropping into their account every other week. All she had to do was check their bank statement to see where he was and what he was buying.

At first she'd wanted to follow him. Especially when she'd realized he'd taken a job. But she'd given him space. Thought for sure he'd come home—call.

Six months later when he'd shown up on their doorstep, she'd welcomed him inside. Welcomed him into their bed.

They'd cried a lot that night. More than they had when Cade died.

She'd never seen Dale so vulnerable—so lost—out of control. They'd made love. Slow and desperate. And with their passion spent, they'd clung to each other in the dark until sleep came.

Waking to an empty bed the next morning gutted her as much as Cade's death had. She'd accepted Dale's visit as goodbye and would have let him go if she hadn't ended up pregnant.

The change had been obvious that first day but she'd chosen to ignore it until her sister had insisted she pee on a stick. By then she was over a month along and living in denial. Her sister's encouragement and that little plus sign had given her the slap in the face she needed—the motivation to pull herself together and go after what she wanted.

She'd lost one mate to circumstances beyond her control. She refused to lose the other if she could do something about it.

Of course it had taken her a few months to sort her life —*their* life—in the city out. She had to make sure her brother and sister would be okay without her. Had to decide what to ship to Whispering Springs, what to leave behind for Tavia and Tarak. When to give notice at her job and when to make the journey home.

Her plan had been to arrive the week after New Year but when the men arrived two days ago to pack their things, she couldn't ignore the need to be home. And by home she meant Dale's arms.

"I'm not going to ask any questions. Which if you ask anyone here they'll tell you is a miracle. But if you want to talk, I'm willing to listen," Kat murmured. "Although I have to admit I am *dying* to know what's up with you and our sexy, broody sheriff."

Tatum smiled.

"Anything you tell me would remain between us." Kat's hand found hers and squeezed. "I know we haven't seen each other in years and we weren't exactly BFFs before you moved away but I recognize someone who needs a friend when I see them."

"Thank you."

"You're welcome." Kat squeezed her hand again and let go.

They were both quiet for a few moments before Tatum whispered, "My last name isn't Brant."

"Oh?"

"It's Turner." Tatum sighed. "Sheriff Dale Turner is my husband."

2

DECEMBER 24

"DON'T LOOK at me like that," Dale growled, ripping off his latex gloves and tossing them in the bin.

Steve's expression became an emotionless mask but it was too late; he'd seen the look on his friend's face.

Frustration and anger tangled his nerves. He'd revealed far too much to Steve in the last few hours. He hadn't meant to but Steve had a way of 'not asking' that made you want to answer. He still wanted to.

"It was never about me liking guys." Dale dragged a hand down his face. 'Like' was too tame a word for what had been between him and Cade. He'd never touched Cade in a sexual way. Never wanted to. What they'd had wasn't about sex. Except in every other way that counted, their relationship was that of a mated couple.

"What was it about then?" Steve asked.

Dale sighed. "Tatum."

Steve frowned. "Tatum?"

"Yeah. Tatum."

"I don't—"

"I know you don't. And I can't explain it. Cade was...the other half of me. We couldn't have been closer if we were Siamese twins; we could finish each other's sentences, communicate without words. People joked about it when we were younger, how alike we were, always wanting the same things. Sometimes it seemed as though he was me and I was him, and I know he felt the same. And the second we laid eyes on Tatum, we knew she was ours. We waited years to claim her. Four years of waiting, of worrying about what people would say, knowing once we touched her there would be no going back." He paused his verbal diarrhea to suck in a breath.

It was so hard to explain what was between the three of them. It was something he'd never seen or heard of in coyote mates.

"Humans are so tolerant of alternate lifestyles nowadays that living together, the three of us, was easy in the city. Doing that here, especially with Connelly as sovereign..." Dale shook his head. The city had let them live as they were, without prejudice or persecution. And then it destroyed them.

"That's why you left so abruptly." It wasn't a question and Dale could see his friend joining the dots quickly. "You went after Tatum."

Dale smiled. Just a small curl of his lips. "Yeah."

"I never understood why William let his daughter-in-law take her children—his only grandchildren—to the city after his son died."

"Tatum's mother never fully embraced the mountains or coyote life—she never allowed Samuel to change her—and without her husband..." He shrugged. "She mourned Tatum's dad until her own death. Tatum thinks, and I agree, she died of a broken heart."

"And you and Tatum broke when Cade died."

Dale grimaced. They'd done more than break. They'd shattered into so many pieces he still couldn't find them all. Wasn't sure he'd ever be able to.

"I don't get what you've been through so I won't pretend I do, but I can imagine, and loving Doc makes that all the more realistic for me so I understand why you came home. What I don't understand is why you didn't bring Tatum with you in the first place. Why you went back only to leave her again."

"I never meant to leave a second time. And I was going back," he muttered.

"When?"

"Last week in January." Half his mouth kicked up when he thought about what he'd planned. "I was going to get her, drag her home kicking and screaming if I had to."

"I take it you didn't know about the babies before we found her crumpled in my driveway?"

"Fuck no! I'd have gone for her before now if I had." Dale shook his head, the surprise of seeing Tatum large with their children still a sucker punch to the gut. "We'd tried for years to have kids. From the moment she married me, Cade and I spent every minute we could trying to knock her up."

"I know it's no consolation, but sometimes things just aren't meant to happen when you want them to. Timing is everything."

Dale looked at Steve. If anyone knew about the right time, it was Steve. He'd watched his mate take another man as her husband only for Doc to leave the mountains for years after the man she'd married and her unborn child died. In some ways they'd been through similar experiences.

Steve clapped him on the shoulder. "C'mon. Let's finish up

here and head over to the Den. Maybe a slice of Kat's double choc chocolate cake will make things better."

"Jesus. What are we? Teenage girls?" Dale grumbled. Although he wouldn't turn down a slice of Kat's legendary double choc cake. He just wasn't going to admit it out loud.

It took them another thirty minutes to wrap everything up at Doc's house. Dale sent his deputies to the station to log the evidence and file their reports. He'd do his later. After he got Tatum settled at home.

He'd listened to her arguments and let her stay in the apartment above the grocer's last night. She had no clue he'd slept in his car out front and he wasn't about to enlighten her. He wasn't telling her he had a key to her front door either.

When he'd first returned to town, he'd lived in the very apartment she'd organized to rent indefinitely. He'd only moved out when Steve had built his house up the mountain leaving his place in town open for new occupants. Since before he'd taken his trip to the city six months ago Dale had been redecorating rooms, adding touches he knew Tatum would like.

After almost a year of renovating old cabinets and installing new appliances. Months of ripping up threadbare carpet and replacing it or sanding hardwood floors, scraping walls and slapping on new paint. He finally had everything the way he thought she'd like and now he had to redo one of the rooms to accommodate their babies.

Dale smiled. He couldn't be mad about the extra work. Madly happy, yes, but angry mad? Definitely not.

He wanted to see her reaction to the things he'd done, the improvements he'd made so far. And now that she was here, she could guide him in outfitting the nursery.

Yep. Tonight she'd stay with him and if she still insisted on staying in her apartment he'd camp on her doorstep instead of freezing his ass off in his car if she wouldn't let him take the couch. From now on, they'd be living under the same roof. Like a husband and wife expecting their first children should be.

Parking behind Steve in front of the cafe, Dale hopped out and met the other man on the snow-dusted sidewalk. Rubbing his bare hands together, he blew on them and said, "Wow. It must have dropped ten degrees."

"Tomorrow's snowstorm is meant to drop temps to minus five," Steve said as he pushed the door to the Den open.

"They're predicting a bad one." Warm air enfolded him as he stepped inside. Dale scanned the tables but didn't see Tatum. "I've had my deputies making sure the older members of the community have all they need for a few days of being snowed in."

"I'll take getting snowed in as long as it's not as destructive as the series of storms we had two years ago."

"I'll second that. I wasn't here for the storm but I saw the aftermath and the repairs being carried out." Making their way to the counter, they took a couple of stools. "Do you want to check the roof at the clinic again before you head home?" he asked Steve.

"No. We'll do that before she opens up again though. I want it checked before she goes back there," Steve said.

Kat place a mug in front of each of them, and asked, "Can I get you something to eat?" as she filled the cups with steaming coffee.

"No, thanks, coffee's fine. Where's Doc?" Steve asked.

"She and Tatum walked over to the clinic to get something for Tatum."

Dale froze, mug halfway to his mouth, and stared at Kat.

Steve jumped from his seat and headed for the door, growling over his shoulder, "Alone? You let them go alone?"

"What's wrong? She said you'd checked it this morning. That it was safe," Kat protested.

"We did." Steve pulled the door open. "But I don't want her going there alone."

Dale didn't bother saying anything; he didn't want any of the women—especially Tatum—alone until Marcus Connelly was caught.

The trouble with Marcus should have stopped weeks ago when he'd driven his truck off Stattler Bridge. Kidnapping the sovereign's mate and leaving her to die alone in the mountains wasn't enough for the exiled pack member, no he had found a way to rise from the dead and terrorize their women once more.

That stopped now. Dale would see to it that Marcus left the pack for good if it was the last thing he did.

Determined to see to the safety of Doc and Tatum, Dale followed right behind Steve, his heart pounding in his chest, in his ears, as every worst-case scenario filled his head. They hit the sidewalk and sprinted across the street without looking.

Sliding to a stop at the clinic door, Steve yanked on the handle, thumped on the door, shouting, "Doc."

Call it instinct or whatever, but he grabbed Steve's arm. "Wait. Listen."

The door muffled the cry but Dale heard enough for every drop of blood in his veins to turn to ice.

"That doesn't sound like Doc," Steve said.

Dale pressed his ear to the door. Hoped he hadn't heard what his coyote was telling him he had. But the cry that came next was loud and clear.

"What the fuck? Tatum!" he yelled, hammering on the door with both fists.

Steve took off down the street.

"Where are you going?" Dale called out as he shook the doorknob in a vain attempt to get inside.

"Around the back."

Dale gave up on the front door and raced after Steve.

"We'll never break down the front door but there's a window above the back one," Steve yelled over his shoulder.

He knew the window. It was nowhere near big enough for either of them to get through but the back wall was timber. They could break that with a couple of well-placed kicks. He'd drive his squad car through it if he had to.

It turned out they didn't need the window or muscle or his car. The rear door was cracked a few inches.

Unholstering his gun, he moved around Steve, and said, "Let me go in first."

"Fine, but I'm right behind you."

He entered the dim hallway slowly. Listening intently, he tried to determine where in the clinic Tatum was. When they reached the morgue, Dale's gut clenched.

Doc lay curled on her side facing away from them, a huge pool of blood coating the floor around her and the man dressed head to toe in black lying on his stomach between her and the door.

Dale had no doubt who the man was.

Steve went to Doc while he checked Marcus.

"I can't find where she's bleeding," Steve choked, his hands frantically moving over Doc, his panic palpable.

"I'm not sure it's her blood." Dale took in the scene. "He's dead, looks like she slashed his throat."

"Jesus. What the fuck happened?" Steve tapped Doc's cheek. "Doc? Come on, Gordie, talk to me," he pleaded.

"I'll be back. I need to find Tatum." Dale held his gun in front of him even though his gut said he wouldn't need it. Instinct told him Marcus had worked alone.

Back in the hall, a few feet deeper into the clinic, a sound from behind had him spinning around, aiming his weapon. Registering old Doc Monroe and Mrs. Monroe, Dale lowered his gun and nodded toward the morgue. "In there."

Satisfied Steve would get the help he needed, Dale moved through the clinic toward the front door, checking each room as he went. Other than the morgue, nothing was disturbed and the only noise came from the rear of the clinic where Steven and the Monroes were taking care of Doc.

As he stepped into the reception area, the sight of Tatum crumpled against the far wall had Dale sprinting across the room and dropping to his knees. "Tay!" Placing his gun on the floor beside him, he searched for possible injuries.

"S-okay." She moaned, her head rolling toward him. "Fainted."

He pulled her up into his arms. "Fuck. Tay." Cradling her against his chest, he rocked, his heart pounding against his ribs —inside his skull—hard enough to hurt.

"Doc?" she mumbled.

"Steve's with her." He wasn't telling her anything else. Not that he knew Doc's condition, but Tatum didn't need to concern herself with that just yet. Not when she went limp in his arms and her head flopped to the side.

Holding her close, he climbed to his feet, and made his way back to the morgue and medical help. His basic first-aid training didn't feel sufficient for this situation.

Entering the room, Dale couldn't stop his voice from quivering when he spoke. "Doctor Monroe?"

"Jesus, Mary, and Joseph. What went on here?" The old man turned to his wife. "Jackie, go with Dale and see about that one for me. I'll bring Gordana in a minute."

Brogan and Quinn burst through the back door as Dale reentered the hallway.

"What do you need us to do, Sheriff?" Brogan asked, coming toward him.

Dale hadn't even thought about his role as sheriff and right now he didn't care if his lack of professionalism got him fired. All that mattered was the semi-conscious woman in his arms.

"A couple of deputies pulled up as we came inside," Quinn offered.

He needed to think... "They'll need to secure the scene... collect evidence." There was something else he needed to tell them... Except it was too hard to think of anything but Tatum. "Oh. My gun. It's on the floor where I found Tatum. Out front. In reception."

Quinn moved around them saying, "On it," as he passed.

Brogan gripped Dale's shoulder, gave him a squeeze. "Take care of Tatum. We'll take care of everything else."

He nodded and let Mrs. Monroe guide him into an exam room. Lowering Tatum to the bed in spite of every instinct screaming at him not to let her go, Dale reluctantly moved out of the way. He had to so she could get the attention she needed. But he didn't leave her side; he remained close, his hip pressed to the bed, his hands holding one of hers.

Mrs. Monroe seemed to understand his need to be near because she worked around him when she had to, checking Tatum's limbs for possible breaks, her head for bumps, her eyes with one of those tiny lights.

It seemed like years but was probably not even a minute before Tatum roused enough to talk to them. Mrs. Monroe asked questions and Tatum answered, her voice growing stronger with every word.

As Tatum revealed what had happened, he became more and more glad Marcus was dead. If he wasn't Dale couldn't be sure he'd be able to stop himself from grabbing his gun and shooting the man.

"How's Doc?" Tatum asked.

Mrs. Monroe's gaze met his. "Her dad is taking care of her." The non-answer seemed to appease Tatum.

"And..." She swallowed, licked her bottom lip. "Marcus?"

"Dead," Dale growled, his hands tightening around hers.

She glanced up at him, a world of emotion in those green eyes of hers. "Dead?"

Mrs. Monroe distracted Tatum from further questions by saying, "All right, let me check on that baby."

"Babies," they said in unison, their gazes locked together.

Dale stared down at his wife. It was a small thing, except they'd done that all the time in the past—spoken the exact same thing at the exact same time—back when they weren't this fractured version of themselves. The smile gracing Tatum's lips delivered another bubble of hope.

They could do this. They could find their way back to each other, could learn to be a duo instead of a trio.

He'd do anything—everything—to make it happen.

A *thump thump thump* beat broke into his thoughts and the silence of the room.

"There now, that's one..." Mrs. Monroe moved the instrument she pressed to Tatum's bare belly to the other side.

Thump thump thump.

The older woman smiled. "And there's two."

"They sound fine," Tatum said, her words filled with certainty.

"They do." Mrs. Monroe switched off the device and reached for another. "I'm going to take your blood pressure now you've had a chance to settle some. All that excitement is bound to have it a little high."

She went to work but Dale couldn't pay attention. All he could think about were those little beating hearts inside Tatum. He knew they were real. He'd felt them moving the other night except hearing them...

He closed his eyes and thanked the universe they were okay—that Tatum appeared to be okay.

"Dale?"

Opening his eyes, he found Mrs. Monroe looking at him with a knowing smile. "You can take Tatum home whenever you're ready. I'll have Doctor Monroe give you a call later but other than a couple of bruises, she and the babies are fine. Plus Tatum knows what to do if anything changes."

He swallowed, the lump in his throat all but choking him. "T-thank you."

She patted his arm, her smile growing wider. "You're welcome."

Together they helped Tatum to her feet and Dale wrapped an arm around her waist to be sure she stayed on them. She didn't argue and he hoped that meant she'd be as compliant when he took her home.

3

TATUM LEANED into Dale as they left the exam room. She was a bit shaky on her legs but had nothing worse than a few aches and pains. Thankfully she hadn't slammed into the wall when Marcus had shoved her aside; she'd rolled along it before sliding to the floor and fainting.

"Hey, you okay?"

Glancing up, she saw Steve coming toward them; a frown furrowed his brow and pulled the edges of his mouth down. She had no idea what had happened after she'd passed out and the little information she'd received from Dale and Mrs. Monroe didn't set her mind to rest. She'd left poor Doc on her own to fight off a madman.

"Yeah, a little embarrassed at passing out and not helping Doc, but otherwise I'm good."

"I'll talk to you later, Steve," Dale said. "I'm taking Tatum home to rest. Brogan and Quinn arrived a little while ago. They're handling the Marcus issue with the help of my deputies."

"Need me to do anything?"

"No. Just take care of Doc."

Dale turned them toward the back door and ushered her outside. The cold air didn't bother her; her nerves, still in shock, were numb, and she couldn't feel much of anything except Dale's strong arm wrapped around her. And a sudden welling of relief to be out of the clinic.

"Shit," Dale muttered as he brought them to a stop a few feet from the door.

She looked up to see what the problem was but couldn't find anything to warrant his curse. "What?"

"My truck is parked in front of the Den."

"It's only around the corner."

"You're not walking that far."

Before she could protest she was fine and could walk the short distance around the buildings, he'd scooped her up in his arms, snuggled her against his chest as though she were a baby, and headed down the alley.

"*Dale.*"

"*Tatum,*" he mimicked her tone, his lips curled up on one side.

She rolled her eyes. "Put me down."

"No."

"You heard Mrs. Monroe, I'm fine. I can walk."

"Probably."

"Then put me down."

"I will." His stride didn't slow, if anything his steps got longer, faster.

"Now."

"Soon."

"For god's sake, Dale."

He chuckled. "God ain't gonna help you."

"Stubborn man."

"Yep."

"I really am okay."

"I know." He glanced down, his gaze awash with emotion. "Just give me this. Please."

It was the please that got her. And the look in his eyes. There was fear swirling in their caramel depths. "Fine. But don't get used to carrying me around."

"We'll see."

She huffed out a breath. "Stubborn."

"Yep."

Tatum didn't need to look at him to know he was smiling; it permeated every letter of that one word. With a sigh, she closed her eyes and laid her head on his shoulder. She'd let him have this moment.

Besides, she was tired. A permanent state lately, but she knew the drop in adrenaline from earlier had a hand in making her drowsy.

She must have dozed off because the next thing she knew, Dale was lifting her out of the passenger seat of his car. And they were inside an unfamiliar garage. "Where are we?"

"Home."

He didn't elaborate and when he moved through a doorway into the house he didn't point out anything. No tour for her. Instead he moved quickly along a dim hallway and into what had to be the master bedroom.

Lowering her to her feet, he said, "Let's get you out of your clothes and into a warm shower."

She was exhausted enough to let him take care of her. Without protest, Tatum allowed Dale to remove her clothes and usher her into the adjoining bathroom. He'd tended to her rarely in her life—she could count those times on one hand.

She'd missed his gruff care. He loved her, she knew that; he'd told her every day, shown her in little ways, except she'd always been so independent and self-sufficient that the times she needed him to care for her completely were few. She treasured them more because of how infrequent they were.

Until a year ago she'd been sure of their future. Now things were complicated, fractured, and even if they could pull it back together it wouldn't be the same. Nothing would be the same without Cade but they needed to find a way.

For the sake of their babies, they needed to work out how to be *now*.

How to be Dale and Tatum.

And they had to do it before the babies came.

DALE WATCHED TATUM SLEEP. He'd managed to get her showered and into bed before she'd completely conked out.

That had been about thirty minutes ago.

She lay on her side, a little restless now, her legs moving around as though she were trying to find a comfortable position. He'd been tempted to leave the covers off her so he could see if the babies moved except the house was still on the chilly side. He'd turned the heat up and it would soon be warm enough for her to go without covers but for now, she lay beneath the quilt Grammy Brant had dropped off a few months ago.

He hadn't realized what the old lady was doing the first few times she'd appeared on his doorstep bearing a gift. She'd called by four times before he'd put the pieces together. It was the quilt that did it.

A hand-stitched wedding ring quilt.

As far as Dale knew, the senior Brants had never been told of their marriage or about the trio they'd formed with

Cade. The old couple had visited them in the city a handful of times over the years, which had surprised Dale. He hadn't thought William would leave the mountains. But the old man made an exception for his only grandchildren.

Cade's funeral was the last time the senior Brants had made the trip down the mountain.

A few months later when Dale had turned up here, in Whispering Springs, without Tatum or her siblings, the old man had patted him on the back and told him everything would work out the way it was supposed to. William hadn't asked any questions, hadn't offered any further advice.

From that first day Grammy Brant—Dale had no idea what her first name was, for as long as he could remember everyone called her Grammy—had become a regular visitor, straightening things up if needed and leaving him food and a gift of some kind each time she showed up on his doorstep.

He'd felt uncomfortable around them at first. It didn't take long for that discomfort to disappear though. The Brants had always welcomed him. And they either didn't know about Tatum's pregnancy or...

"I need to ring Grammy," Tatum murmured.

Jesus, was she reading his mind? Had he been talking out loud?

"It can wait." He brushed the hair from her face. "Rest."

"She'll worry."

"Okay. You sleep. I'll call her." He pushed to his feet.

"They know."

Pausing, he gazed down at a sleepy-eyed Tatum. "Know what?"

She smiled. "Everything."

"Oh."

Closing her eyes, she said, "They've always known."

"*Always?*" He felt his eyes go wide and his eyebrows shoot up into his hair line as he stared down at her.

Smiling, she opened her eyes again. "I told them the year I turned thirteen that I'd found my mates. I think that was why Gramps was so upset when Mom took us away after Dad died."

A flash of memory. Of William coming to him and Cade, telling them his daughter-in-law was taking the children away. Jesus. The old man had encouraged them to follow. Had helped pack up their old truck. And Tatum's mother hadn't seemed surprised to find them at her door.

Shit. So much of the past began to make sense.

He brushed a finger down her cheek. "I'll call them now."

Her eyelids lowered and Dale watched for a few seconds, making sure she'd drifted off to sleep again before leaving the room to make the call.

The doorbell rang as he stepped into the kitchen. Thinking it would be Brogan or Quinn, he hurried to answer it. Except it wasn't the pack's sovereign or regal on his doorstep. It was the Brants.

Opening the door wide, he gestured them in out of the cold. "She's okay," he reassured them. "Tired. A few bruises but she and the babies are fine."

Grammy enfolded him in a crushing hug and the full impact of his words finally hit him. He shuddered in her arms, relief and gratitude swamping him. Closing his eyes, he held the old woman close. She patted his back, rubbed soothing circles, and let him take comfort in her arms.

Gathering himself, Dale pulled back. "Sorry."

"Nonsense, boy. Nothing beats a good hug." She smiled up at him. "Now, let me get this soup on the stove. It's already made, only needs a little heating up."

Dale hadn't noticed the big pot William carried when he'd let them in, but with the other man's arms full, Dale didn't offer a hand to shake; instead he ushered them into the kitchen.

"I've spoken to Brogan," William said as he placed the huge pot on the cooktop. "With it being Christmas tomorrow and that big storm heading our way, we'll convene a council meeting after the New Year."

"I should—"

"Nonsense." Grammy lit the burner and took the lid off the pot. The room instantly filled with a delicious aroma and Dale's stomach growled. "You need to be here taking care of your wife. Your deputies are capable, and our sovereign and regal can take care of anything they can't for now."

He'd frozen at the word wife. Unsure whether to acknowledge the comment or not, he stood still, his mind swirling with a million possible things to say.

"William. Keep an eye on this while I go check on Tatum," Grammy ordered.

Dale watched her leave the kitchen and head straight for the master bedroom. She'd been here often enough she knew her way around so he didn't need to tell her or show her where to find Tatum.

"She's a force of nature that one. Not unlike our Tatum."

William's words had Dale turning back to the older man. "I..." He didn't know what to say. How to explain. *What* to explain. Rubbing a hand down his face, he sighed.

William chuckled. "Don't tie yourself in knots. I told you everything would work out the way it was supposed to."

"Not with any help from me," he muttered.

"Sometimes we have to take the long way round to get to where we're going."

Dale could understand that, but could they get to where they were going when one of them was gone?

Proving Dale was easy to read or William was a mind

reader, the old man said, "You were never meant to get to the end together. As much as it pains me to say it, Cade wasn't meant to be with you here. Take comfort in the time you all had. It's better to have had than not."

"Doesn't feel that way."

"The children will help with that."

He groaned. "I've fucked up so much."

The old man grinned. "We all fuck up once in a while."

"But I hurt Tay. Over and over. And I left her to cope with her pregnancy on her own."

"You needed time. So did she." William gripped his shoulder and squeezed. "You're both in a better place now. And you're home. Where you were always meant to be."

Home.

The place Cade had refused to visit. He never would have moved back to Whispering Springs. Dale couldn't imagine living in the city forever, raising a family there. Hell, the only reason they'd stayed in the city after Tatum's mom died was because Cade wouldn't return to the mountains.

Cade had thrived in the city. Loved working the dark streets, being a cop in a large metropolis. He'd have been bored out of his brain working as a small town cop and yet Dale loved it. Loved knowing all the people in his territory. Cade would have hated that. He'd liked the anonymity of city life where Dale had found it disconnected—isolating.

Maybe they hadn't been so alike after all.

TATUM PLACE her empty bowl on the timber chest masquerading as a coffee table and leaned back on the lumpy sofa with a sigh. She was so exhausted, she didn't care about the hard thing digging into her left butt cheek. "That was delicious."

"Do you want more? There's plenty." Dale picked up her bowl and climbed to his feet. "Grammy left us the whole pot."

"Maybe later." She watched as he made his way to the kitchen with their dirty dishes.

She'd woken a little while ago, the smell of Grammy's homemade chicken soup teasing her senses. Finding Dale, lying beside her, his head propped in his hand, his eyes glued to her face had momentarily given her pause. Then she'd smiled.

He used to watch her sleep all the time. Said he couldn't get enough of seeing her breathing whether asleep or awake.

Kat had been right in her description of Dale. He was broody, but only because he didn't waste words. If he didn't have anything to say, he didn't bother with small talk. That had been Cade's skill.

Out of the three of them, Cade had been the social one. Dale had been the tall, dark, and silent one. And she'd fallen somewhere in between the two.

It wasn't that she or Dale were anti-social. They just preferred to keep their circle small, close. Whereas Cade had never met anyone he hadn't treated like a lifelong friend. She had to wonder if that trait contributed to his death.

They'd never talked about what had happened. Dale hadn't wanted to burden her with the details. All she knew was Cade had been shot in the chest and bled out before help could arrive. She had no clue if he might have survived if that help had come sooner. Or if the kid who'd shot him hadn't kept police and paramedics out of that alley by firing at anyone who tried to get near.

Perhaps they needed to talk about what happened to Cade. Get everything out in the open so they could work their way through the grief, the incomprehensible events of that night, and finally put it behind them.

"Hey."

Glancing up she found Dale standing beside her, a frown on his face. She smiled and answered, "Hey, yourself."

"You okay? Want to talk about what happened?" he asked as he sat on the couch next to her.

She did want to talk, but not about what he thought. "Yes. I want to talk."

"All right." He turned so he was facing her head-on. "I'm listening."

"What happened the night Cade died?"

To his credit, Dale didn't flinch but she felt him stiffen, every muscle in his body going rigid, frozen in place. He sucked in a deep breath and let it out slowly. "He was shot three times."

"I know that. I want to know what happened. Why he was there, alone, without backup. Without *you*."

She'd never understood that part. Cade and Dale had been partners. They'd worked every case together, and if not, there was always another detective to go with them. It was a rule of their precinct—no officer went out alone.

Dale closed his eyes on a sigh. "He wouldn't wait. Said he knew the kid, he was harmless. Low man in the organization of the dealer we were after. Cade had been trying for weeks to turn the kid into an informant."

"But neither of you were on shift." Another thing she hadn't understood. Why had Cade gone out while off duty?

"No. We were home with you when he got the call from the kid. He told Cade he had some information he wanted." Dale opened his eyes. "I'll never forgive myself for letting him talk me into staying home."

"Do you think he knew something was off?" When it first

happened, she'd wondered if Cade had been set up with the way the kid had barricaded the alley and kept everyone away.

"No. He honestly thought it was no big deal and perfectly safe."

"Then what went wrong? You know more than you've told me. I'm not fragile, Dale, and I need to understand so I can move forward." If he wouldn't tell her, she'd do the one thing she'd stopped herself from doing all this time. She'd go to their old precinct and ask.

"It was a setup of sorts. The kid was proving he had what it took to move up the ladder within the drug network. Of course he ended up dead as well. The network didn't want him snitching so they had someone shank him."

She knew the teenager had died in custody. Some sort of fight between inmates. She'd had no clue he'd been targeted by the people he'd worked for. "Such a waste."

"There was one good thing to come out of what happened."

"Oh?"

Dale nodded. "The kid's mother took her younger boys away from the city. Back to the small town she'd grown up in. Last time I checked, the three boys were proving that environment matters. They're all doing well in school and heading in the opposite direction of their dead brother."

"There's no father?"

He shook his head. "No. Hasn't been in the picture since the youngest was born."

"I can't imagine how that woman must feel." She smoothed a hand over her belly. Watching the child you raised succumb to a gang, deal drugs, murder a policeman... Tatum couldn't even begin to comprehend the emotions the woman was dealing with.

"She's as much a victim of her son's actions as Cade was.

Luckily she has the opportunity to rebuild. Change the course of her other children's lives."

"Cade would like that. To know that she took her younger boys out of the city and away from the streets and the drug and gang culture that's so rampant."

"He would."

"Do you think we could help her? Maybe give her an anonymous donation of school supplies? A year of groceries or clothes for her growing boys? I haven't touched Cade's life insurance."

"If that's what you want to do with the money. But I thought you would want to use it for the babies."

"I'll put some aside for them but it's a lot of money, Dale. There's more than enough to go around."

The amount still astounded her. Even Dale hadn't known Cade had taken out such a large policy. When the lawyer had first contacted them about it, Tatum had thought it was a mistake. Except when all the paperwork and Cade's will had been finalized, they'd received a check for a million dollars.

Dale scrubbed a hand over his face. "I can't believe he never said he changed the payout on his insurance."

"I can't either, but when I think about it, it's such a Cade thing to do."

"Yeah, like going off on his own to meet a small-time drug dealer in an alley."

"He could be wildly reckless and super cautious depending on his mood." She smiled. "He did everything to the extreme, didn't he?"

"I never thought so before that night."

Tatum shrugged. "I guess we were so used to who he was that we didn't see it."

"Or overlooked it because we loved him," Dale murmured.

"We did love him."

Dale's hand slipped over hers, his fingers curling under to press into her palm. "We loved each other too," he whispered. "Cade might not be here but that doesn't mean the love is gone."

She turned to look at him. There was so much emotion in his gaze her tummy dipped. "The only thing that died was Cade. I still love him." Tatum smiled, her eyes filling, her bottom lip trembling. "I still love you, Dale."

4

DALE SUCKED in a breath and held it as Tatum's words wrapped around his heart and squeezed. He didn't deserve her love. He'd abandoned her when he should have protected her—supported her. Instead of running away to get his head on straight, he should have held her close, leaned on her to help him through his grief.

"I'm sorry." He reached up and brushed a finger over her cheekbone. "I should never have left."

"No. You needed to get out of the city, I understand that, but you should have talked to me. Taken me with you."

He closed his eyes. "Yes. I should have."

"Next time."

His eyes shot open. "No. There won't be a next time. I'm never leaving you again, Tay. You have my word on that."

She smiled. "Just so you know, if you did go, I'd follow."

"You already did."

"Ha. Not at first."

"I don't think badly of you because you didn't come after me. Not with the way I left."

"I was mad about that in the beginning. But as the days passed and I thought about where you were, I knew you'd gone where you needed to be. When you came back then left again... well, I figured that was goodbye. I was really mad then. So angry I tried to ignore the changes in my body, to my scent, until Tavia said something. Her words and the pregnancy test she shoved into my hands helped me face reality. And then I knew I couldn't accept that as goodbye. If you were done with me, I needed to hear you say it."

"I'll never be done with you."

"Good."

"How about this? If either of us feels the need to go, for any reason, we say so. No more hiding how we feel or what we're thinking. I know that should be a given between mates but our mating was different than others and I think we, *I*, let that difference get in the way of what we are to each other. I hope you can forgive me, Tay, but I promise you, I'll spend every day for the rest of my life making it up to you."

"There's nothing to forgive. I know you; you didn't deliberately set out to hurt me. We were both in a bad place after Cade, struggling to find our way, not knowing how to reach each other. We let ourselves forget the most important thing we had. Each other. Instead we focused on what we'd lost."

"Cade."

A small smile curved her lips. "Yes. Cade."

"Come here." He pulled her into his arms and snuggled her against his chest. "I'll never forget what we have again," he promised.

"I don't love you because I loved Cade. I love you for you, Dale. My connection to each of you is separate and not reliant on the other."

"I didn't think it was. Except so much of myself was tied up in my connection to Cade. For so long I've thought of him as part of me. It took me a while to understand I'm still me without him. And recently I've discovered things weren't as I thought. We weren't exactly the same. If the situation had been reversed, he never would have come back here; the mountains would be the last place he'd seek solace."

"I never understood why he hated it here."

"It had something to do with when he was little, before I knew him, I think. He never told me how he came to live with the Bakers."

"They were a weird old couple. Gramps used to tell me to stay away from them. I think that's why he used to find work for you and Cade to do. So Cade wouldn't have to be at their house much."

"Your Gramps has a way of manipulating things. Did you know he encouraged us to follow you to the city? Even helped us pack our stuff, gave us gas money." Dale shook his head; he'd forgotten about the five hundred dollars William had pressed into his hand before they'd left Whispering Springs.

"He's a crafty old thing." Tatum yawned around her words.

"C'mon, let's get you back to bed." He pushed to his feet taking her with him. Snuggling her as close as he could with her belly in the way, he asked, "Do you need anything? A glass of water?"

"No. I'll be up all night peeing if I drink anything now." She went to move away from him and he tightened his grip.

"Let me help you."

"I'm fine, Dale."

"I know. I'd still like to help you." He wanted to carry her except he knew she'd argue against that. If all he could get was an arm around her shoulders, he'd take it.

"Don't coddle me."

"I'm not coddling you," he said as he steered her down the hallway to the bedroom. "I'm coddling me. I swear, seeing you crumpled on the floor stopped my heart. It might take me a few days to recover from that shock."

She glanced up at him. "I'm tough. If I wasn't harboring a couple of parasites I'd have given Marcus a run for his money."

Dale shuddered as ice drenched his veins. He had no doubt she would have. Just the thought of it took his breath and kicked his heart into overdrive. Tightening his arms around her, he muttered, "Thanks for putting those images in my head. I was already guaranteed nightmares; now I don't think I'm brave enough to close my eyes at all."

They entered the bedroom and Tatum headed for the bathroom. "I need to empty out before I lie down or I'll be up within the hour."

She didn't need to explain. He figured she'd want to use the bathroom before hopping into bed. While Tatum took care of things, Dale turned down the bedcovers. She'd made the bed when she'd woken. Smiling he remember the numerous arguments they'd had over the years about making the bed. He didn't see the point when you were only going to mess it up again.

"Aren't you coming to bed?" Tatum asked.

He hadn't heard her. She'd managed to get right behind him without him noticing. "I...um..." Glancing over his shoulder at her, he said, "You want me to sleep with you?"

She cocked her head to the side, her eyes narrowing. "Why wouldn't I?"

"Oh, well." He scratched his head. "I thought..."

Her laughter filled the room. "You should see your face. The last time I saw that look was our wedding night."

Memories bombarded him, his body instantly reacting to the vivid images. "I haven't felt this nervous around you and a bed since that night."

"Dale. I'm six months pregnant with your babies. I think we can sleep in the same bed without difficulty."

"Are you sure?"

Sighing, she muttered, "Dumbass," as she walked around him.

"Hey."

"Hey yourself." She climbed onto the mattress and pulled the covers over her belly. "We're either making this work or we're not."

"Of course we are."

"Then, *husband*, come to bed with your *wife*."

Dale stared at Tatum. She always managed to surprise him. "I didn't want to push."

"Push all you want—" a yawn cut off her words. "Jeez. I'm exhausted. You'd think I hadn't woken from a two hour nap less than an hour ago."

"Another reason I shouldn't—"

"Dale Turner, get your stubborn ass in this bed and hold me until I fall asleep, then you can climb out if sleeping with me is so repulsive."

"What? No! Fuck, Tay. I'd love nothing more than to crawl in beside you and hold you all night but I don't want to fuck this up any more than I already have."

"The only way you'll fuck things up further is if you don't get in here." She flipped back the covers and patted the bed beside her. "Promise I won't jump you."

He laughed. "Now that I'd love to see. You can barely walk straight with those two filling your belly."

Her lips stretch into a smile so blinding Dale had to blink. "See, nothing to fear from the ungainly pregnant woman."

"You're beautiful."

Tipping her head down, she fluttered her lashes, and said, "Flattery will get you everywhere."

Shucking his pants, he left his boxers and t-shirt on, and moved around the bed. He'd wanted to be under the same roof as her; being in the same bed was far more than he deserved. He hadn't begun to make amends for the pain he'd caused her. Dale wasn't about to refuse the invitation though. He might be a dumbass but he wasn't stupid.

He slipped under the covers and moved toward her. "Come here."

She wiggled over, burrowing into his side; her body curved around the babies, she pressed her face into the side of his neck the way she'd done so many times in the past. Arms wrapped around her, Dale took a deep breath and savored the woman in his arms.

He'd almost destroyed them by leaving her behind. He wouldn't make that mistake again. Now that she'd given him a chance to make things right he planned to make them so right she never thought about their time apart again.

5

DECEMBER 25

TATUM STARED out at the storm, her insides churning in a mix of pleasure and fear. Pleasure because she hadn't been in the mountains for a snowstorm in years and fear because this was a doozy and Dale was out in it.

He'd gotten a call right after lunch. About ten minutes after the power had gone out. He'd already started the generator before being alerted to the storm damage by his deputy so she had heat and could use the lights. The stovetop was gas, so she'd rummaged around in the kitchen and found the ingredients to put on a batch of spaghetti sauce. It'd be ready no matter when Dale came home.

Home.

She glanced around. The tour he hadn't given her yesterday had happened this morning. With each room he took her through she could see the care he'd put into it. She could feel the love in every refurbished inch of the place.

That he'd done it for her—for them—well, she'd gotten a little teary over that. Pregnancy hormones hadn't just turned her into an exhausted blimp. They'd made her a leaky faucet. It didn't take much to bring her to tears nowadays, and Dale's care and thoughtfulness, the love he lavished on every inch of this place with her in mind, only cemented her belief in them.

He'd made them a home.

The house they'd had in the city had belonged to her mother and although the place had come to her and her siblings on her mother's death, no one had bothered to redecorate. Even the curtains were the same ones her mother had put up when they'd first moved in almost a decade ago.

This house was their first real home. Dale had told her he'd bought it from Steve and had planned to bring her here six months ago. He'd cut his words off at that; she wasn't sure what he hadn't wanted to tell her and wasn't sure if she should ask. Except she wanted to know.

Needed to know why he'd come back to her only to leave again.

It was the one thing they hadn't discussed yet. The last thing she needed to understand so they—*she*—could really move forward. Not that she was going anywhere.

Nope. She was here to stay.

She was fighting for what they had. Dale still loved her, had never stopped loving her, and she'd certainly never stopped loving him.

Light flashed through the falling snow and the sound of the garage door opening vibrated through the house. Pulling the blanket around her shoulders tighter, Tatum made her way to the connecting door and waited for Dale to come inside. She didn't want to open the door and let out all the warm air so she leaned against the wall opposite until he appeared.

"Hey." He stepped in from the garage, unzipping his thick

jacket. "Tree took out the substation. No power 'til the snow lets up and the crews can get to it. Phone lines are down too." Hopping on each foot in turn, he yanked off his boots and dropped them on the floor.

He was fully clothed—jeans, sweater, scarf and beanie, thick socks, with one big toe poking out—and yet he may as well be naked for the way her body reacted. He hadn't done anything remotely sensual as he removed his outer layer but that didn't seem to matter. Every nerve quivered with excitement. It appeared him stripping out of his jacket and boots was enough to awaken her libido.

"You okay?" he asked as he stepped closer.

"Uh-huh."

He eyed her. "Tay?"

"It's just pregnancy hormones."

Frowning, he asked, "What is?"

"Anything, everything. It's always pregnancy hormones."

"O...kay." He moved even closer. "I want to wrap my arms around you except you're flushed with warmth and I'm cold. All the way to the bone cold. I'm gonna jump in a hot shower then I'll see about getting us some dinner."

"I made dinner."

"You did?" One dark eyebrow arched.

Nodding, she stepped into him and murmured, "Want me to wash your back?"

Dale froze, the look on his face making her laugh.

"Does it shock your delicate sensibilities that I want to get naked with you, Sheriff?"

"Ah..."

She trailed a finger down his chest until she reached his utility belt. "Why, Sheriff, is that a..." She patted his buckle. "Gun in your pocket or..." Glancing up through her lashes she saw Dale's throat work as he swallowed, his eyes dilate.

"Tay." The nickname was ground out through clenched teeth.

"Hmm."

"Don't tease me."

Giving up her coy act, she straightened and looked him in the eye. "Who's teasing?"

"Tay," he moaned.

"Sometimes a wife wants to wash her husband's back."

"You need to take it easy." He swallowed again, scrunched his eyes closed for a second as he took a deep breath. "After yesterday."

"Dale, after yesterday I want to make the most of every second. I *need* to make the most of every second." She planted both hands on his chest. "Please. Don't make me beg." She'd begged before. But not like this. Before it had been him driving her so out of her mind she couldn't do anything except beg him.

He eyed her for a few seconds and she thought he would deny her, making her wait until he'd gotten in the shower so she could sneak in behind him. Except he shook his head and blew out a breath. "My way."

"But—"

Two fingers pressed against her mouth. "No. I'm giving in on this; I won't give in on anything else."

"I don't understand," she murmured, her lips rubbing on the rough skin of his fingers.

"I know what you want. It's in your eyes, Tay. It's the look you gave me six months ago. It's one of the reasons I left."

"Oh." He didn't want her to want him?

"C'mon. I need to warm up." He grabbed her hand and tugged her behind him. "Although I'm pretty sure you taking your clothes off will do that if the fire in my groin is anything to go by," he grumbled as he ushered her into the bathroom ahead of him.

The hand on her lower back left her and she spun around to find Dale stripping out of his sweater and thermal. Next went the jeans, underwear, and socks. Jesus, he was a sight for the senses. Arousal shot through her and lit her up. Everything tightened and heated, and dampness slicked her panties.

Completely oblivious to the fire raging inside her, he leaned into the shower stall and flicked a couple of taps. Water poured from the ceiling shower-head as well as several nozzles positioned on one wall.

Without looking at her, he stepped beneath the spray, a shudder rippling down his body, a moan of pleasure rumbling in his throat.

Jesus. He was right. Stripping off clothes shot her temp up another ten degrees. She was sweating and the dampness in her panties became a flood.

"Get in here, Tay," he growled.

Her gaze darted up his body and connected with his. Fire blazed, scorched, and sizzled in his caramel eyes. A shiver worked its way down her spine. Goose bumps broke out on her skin. And muscles, unused in six months, contracted.

"I won't ask again."

She knew he wouldn't. He'd gone all alpha on her and she wasn't about to deny herself the pleasure his demands always brought her. Stripping out of her borrowed sweater and sweat pants, along with her soaking wet underwear—she'd forgone a bra—Tatum walked into the shower and into Dale's arms.

One of them moaned. Maybe both of them did. She couldn't be sure once his mouth crashed down on hers. Everything but the feel of him—wet and hot—pressed against her, invading her mouth, short circuited every synapse, zapped every nerve.

Hands slid over slick flesh. His. Hers. Both searching. Needing. Giving. Taking.

The last time they were together had been frantic—desperate—and now, as the frenzy of their first touches settled, their strokes turned sensual—worshipful.

"God, I missed you, Tay," he spoke against her lips. "I was such a fucking dumbass. Can you ever forgive me?"

"I'm here, Dale."

"Yes." His lips curved against hers. "Yes, you are."

She opened her mouth but the words she wanted to say were swallowed by his kiss. He took it deep, his tongue reaching in for hers, stroking, dueling, commanding. She surrendered willingly.

He'd never had to do more than kiss her to make her quiver with need. Except with her breasts extra sensitive and her hormones on overdrive thanks to her pregnancy, Tatum found herself on the verge of orgasm. His cock pressed into her belly, the huge mound stopping it from getting close to the throbbing need in her pussy.

"Dale," she gasped, tilting her hips toward him. "Please."

He worked out the problem quickly, his hand sweeping over her ass, around her thigh, and between her legs. His fingers stroked, pressed, dipped deeper to collect the slick arousal coating her folds. "You're so close."

"Yes." Panting, she rocked her hips, forced his fingers back and forth over her clit. "*Yes...*" she hissed as her climax detonated.

Pulling her closer with one arm, Dale continued to work her pussy until the pressure became too much and she jerked away. "Easy," he murmured, swirling his fingers lightly over her sensitized flesh. "Ride it out for me."

Following his demands, she let him take her through the final waves of pleasure.

"You're so beautiful when you come," he murmured into her hair. "So hard to resist."

The smile that curved her mouth was more post-orgasmic euphoria than pleasure at his words. She remained limp against him as he maneuvered them to the seat built into the side wall of the shower. He held her up while he positioned himself, then turning her around, he lowered her to his lap until he held her hovering over his cock.

"Put me inside you," he commanded.

She glanced over her shoulder. "Like this?"

"Yes. I can't take you against the wall like I want to on account of the babies."

"Oh." She hadn't thought of that. They hadn't been together for months. Hell, sex hadn't entered her head for months. She'd skimmed over those sections in the pregnancy books she'd bought.

"Tay," he groaned. "Hurry up. You're killing me."

Smiling, she reached down and wrapped her fingers around the base of his shaft. Holding him steady, she let him guide her.

The first touch drew a moan from both of them.

The first inch sucked the air from her lungs and left her insides quivering.

The first deep plunge took her right back up to the peak she'd just tumbled over.

Crying out, she gripped his hands where they cupped her hips and held on. He was strong enough to take control, to take them both on the ride her trembling body seemed to need once more. His teeth scraped over her shoulder, up the curve of her neck until he gripped her earlobe, flicking it with his tongue.

"Come for me again, Tay." His hands tightened. "I want to feel your hot pussy squeezing the cum out of my cock."

Tatum moaned, every muscle wrapped around his erection clenching. "Dale," she pleaded.

Finally he took command of her body and, raising her up

slowly, he tortured them both. "Fast or slow?" he asked and pulled her back down hard. "Both."

He did it again. A slow glide up, hard crash down. Over and over he worked her body with his, drove her quickly to the edge but didn't let her tumble. He loved to hold her on that sharp peak. The razor slice of pleasure that bordered on pain.

"Dale. Please." She clamped her pussy walls around his length.

He grunted in her ear, nipped at her lobe, licked down her neck, and sank his teeth into the curve.

Air left her in a gush as pleasure filled her from head to toe when the sting of his bite set off her climax. Bucking on his lap, she held on, rode out each surge of ecstasy as Dale held her aloft and drove his hips up to slam his cock into her repeatedly.

Warmth flooded her. From the orgasm rolling over her and from the cum spilling inside her.

Dale gasped in her ear. "Tay." His hands left her hips and slid around her belly, cradling her against his chest as their breathing slowed, their heart rates lowering with every gasp.

They sat there, bodies cooling, for long moments. Steam drifted around them, water still flowing.

"Love you," he murmured into her neck.

"Love you too."

"I didn't mean for that to happen."

Tatum laughed. She'd always loved snapping his control. It rarely happened; not the sex, that happened whenever they got naked, but Dale's control was legendary. And she could break it. There was feminine power in that. Satisfaction—maybe a little smugness too—in knowing she could get to him so deeply he let go.

"We should get out." He was still hard inside her.

"Hmm..."

"Tay."

A smile curved her lips. "We're not done yet."

DALE HAD STARTED with good intentions. Then again he *always* started with good intentions when it came to Tatum. He could pinpoint the moment things had gone off the rails today.

The second he'd looked up after dropping his boots.

Fire blazed in her eyes, her breath coming in shallow bursts, and she couldn't have hidden the twin beams pointing out from her chest.

He'd been helpless to resist her.

He always was with Tatum. She was his kryptonite.

Which made his retreat to the mountains confusing.

When he thought he could be all she wanted—needed—he'd gone for her only to fall back into the dark pit of his insecurity all over again.

Being with her without Cade didn't seem possible. He hadn't known how to love her on his own.

He did now.

Loving her was easy. She made it easy.

All he had to do was let it happen. There was no controlling love. They'd learned that when the three of them had discovered their connection all those years ago. Just because there were only two of them now didn't mean that love was any less. If anything, it was more for having loved Cade—been loved by Cade.

She stirred in his arms, making him smile.

She'd declared they weren't done and promptly fallen asleep. The hot water wouldn't run out. One thing he'd learned living in a house with six people. Instant hot water was the only way to go.

"Dale?" Her sleep-slurred confusion made him smile wider.

"Yeah."

"Oh, god." She tried to get off his lap. "I'm sorry. I didn't mean—"

He swiveled her around until she sat sideways and covered her mouth with a hand. "Nothing to be sorry about, Tay."

She smiled against his palm.

Removing his hand he said, "You obviously needed a nap after those two orgasms."

A flush that had nothing to do with the warm air around them filled her cheeks. He loved that she blushed when they talked about sex. Not all the time, but every now and then he could get a nice rosy flush out of her.

She tucked her face into the curve of his neck. "I hate that part of being pregnant."

"You're building little people in there. That's hard work. Plus I think it's the body's way of getting you ready for little to no sleep once they're here. Call it practice napping. You'll need to be an expert by the time they're born."

"I think I hit expert level in week five."

The reminder of all he'd missed—what he'd let her deal with alone—sat heavy in his chest. No more though. From now on, he'd be there every step of the way. Tightening his grip on Tatum, he rose to his feet. "Let's get cleaned up. You said you made dinner."

"Oh. I did."

He steadied her on her feet and reached for the soap. "You also said something about washing my back." Holding out the bar he waited until she took it before turning around.

"Why'd you leave the second time?"

Dale closed his eyes. He'd known she'd ask eventually. At least now he had an answer. Before she'd arrived in Whispering

Springs, he couldn't have told her. As much as he was ready for her to come home, he still hadn't understood what sent him running six months ago.

"Dale?"

Turning around he cradled her face, tipping her head up as he leaned forward to rest his brow on hers. "I freaked out."

"Freaked out? Why?"

"That night. We were so...desperate, needy, and I know you came; I did too but I didn't feel as though I was enough, if the two of us were enough. Cade wasn't there to soothe you after I'd taken—"

"Stop right there." She slammed her hands against his chest, pulled against his hold. "I never *needed* Cade to soothe me or you to take me. I only *needed* you to love me. And with every breath Cade took he did. I know you do too, Dale. It's all I ever need from you. However you want to do it. Demanding, soothing, both, whatever. All I want is for *you* to love me."

"I do. That never changed. Not for one second did that stop."

"Then you're enough. *We* are enough."

He brought her close and pressed his lips to her forehead. "I wish I could go back—"

"If wishes were horses, beggars would ride."

Laughing, he let her go and turned around. "Okay, time to get to work, wife."

In answer to his demand, she slapped his ass. Hard.

"Hey, payback's a bitch, Tay."

"Yeah." Pressing herself against him she muttered, "I'm counting on that."

Fuck. His body tightened. He remembered how much she loved playing. They didn't do it often, and honestly, it wasn't a kink he needed, but he did enjoy it. Tatum had too. And Cade had loved to watch them.

"We can do this without Cade," she whispered into his back.

"I know."

"He'd be really pissed if we didn't."

Dale chuckled then groaned when Tatum reached around and slid her soap-slick hand over his cock. "Yes."

Tatum giggled. "Was that yes to what I said or yes to what I'm doing?"

"Both. Jesus." He sucked in a breath when she quickened her strokes, squeezed him tighter. "Don't stop."

"I don't plan to."

Working her hand up and down, she drove him close to coming in an embarrassingly short amount of time. "Tay," he gasped.

She had two hands on him now. One cupped his balls, the other furiously stroking him from root to tip, with the extra squeeze at the head that he loved.

"I'm going to come," he growled.

"Wait." She moved around in front of him and dropped to her knees, pushed out her chest. "On me. Come on me."

His hands joined hers and together they jerked him off until he sprayed her tits with thick white streams of cum. Shuddering though each pulse, Dale wanted to get on his knees. Wanted to worship at her feet for all she'd put up with, for every wrong he'd ever done her.

6

DECEMBER 31

SIX DAYS.

Tatum couldn't wipe the smile off her face.

Six days of being with Dale and she knew they'd never be apart again. They'd worked their way through more of the past year and a half. Spoken of fears and hopes. She knew they were in a good place. Knew they were where they were supposed to be.

She also knew Cade never would have come here with them, and she could admit, and had done so out loud to Dale, that she never would have been happy raising their family in the city.

"You ready?" Dale slipped his arms around her from behind and stroked her belly.

He did that a lot. Stroked the babies. He talked to them too. He told them all about the mountains and how they were going to love growing up here. They'd made peace with being here—

being without Cade. It still felt like something was missing but it didn't hurt like it had before.

"Tay?" He reached up with one hand and gripped her chin, turned her face away from the snow-covered street in front of their house so he could lean over and look at her. "You okay?"

The concern in his eyes made her smile. "Yeah, just thinking about everything."

"Are you happy?"

"Of course." She wiggled to loosen his hold and turned in his arms; sliding her hands up his chest and over his shoulders, she locked her fingers together behind his neck and stood on her tip-toes so she could press her lips to his before settling back on her heels and asking, "Why would you think I'm not? Isn't the smile I can't seem to wipe off my face a clue to how happy I am?"

"I want to be sure."

"Thank you."

"For?"

"Checking. But we promised we wouldn't hold anything back from now on. No hiding how we feel no matter what it is so you can bet your ass you'll know the second I'm not happy about something."

"Promise?"

"Pinky swear." She held up her hand, pinky cocked ready to link with his.

Smiling, he hooked his finger around hers. "Pinky swear."

Grinning, Tatum pushed to her toes again and kissed him. She'd meant for it to be a quick peck but Dale had other ideas. He thrust his tongue against her lips and forced his way inside. Not that she was objecting. Nope. She loved the way he demanded her response. He'd never truly force her but he'd push until she surrendered or said no. She couldn't imagine a time when she wouldn't surrender to him though. Everything he did was for pleasure. Hers and his.

When he finally let her go, they were both breathing hard and she could see the lust swirling in his eyes. She wanted to strip off her clothes and sate his hunger. Ease the answering need burning inside her.

Dale growled. "Fuck. We don't have time."

He snatched her closer. Slammed his mouth over hers once more. It wasn't enough. Would never be enough but they really had to leave. With a small growl of her own, she pulled away and slipped out of his arms.

"Hold that thought. We'll definitely get back to it. But for now, let's go to a wedding."

"Do you regret ours?"

"No, why would I?"

"We didn't have family or friends there. No celebratory dinner after."

"I had the two most important people there. You and Cade."

"If I haven't said it today, I love you."

"So you should." She hip-checked him and headed for the door before she changed her mind about leaving and dragged him to the floor. "Now come on. I want to get there before Doc and Steve."

"Are we out?"

Stopping, Tatum spun on her heel. "Out?"

"Yeah, you know. Are we telling everyone we're married? About Cade?"

"If it comes up." She paused. "Or do you think we should make an announcement or something?"

"I don't want to overshadow Steve and Doc."

"Oh, no. Definitely not. Okay, so we'll just answer questions if anyone asks."

"If that's what you want."

Smiling she moved back into his arms. "I want the whole world to know we're together."

"They'll know the minute they get a whiff of either of us." Dale laughed.

"Yes, they will." Grabbing a handful of his shirt front, Tatum pulled him down to her and kissed him.

EPILOGUE

FEBRUARY 26

"DALE!"

The scream from the bathroom had Dale falling over his chair in his haste to get to Tatum. Saving himself a busted nose by planting his hands on the floor, he scrambled on hands and feet to the wall and pulled himself upright. He sprinted down the hall and through the bedroom; skidding to a stop in the doorway of their en suite, he found her standing in a puddle in the middle of the room, her grey leggings soaked from the crotch down. "What the—"

"My water," she gasped. "My water broke."

He knew what that meant. And it wasn't that she'd peed herself. "But you're not due for weeks."

"There's two, remember? Twins are often early."

Now she told him. *Fuck.* He wasn't ready.

Sure the nursery was finished and they had everything they needed for when they brought the babies home but...

He wasn't ready!

They couldn't do this yet. "You have to stop it," he blurted out.

Tatum stared at him unblinking for a full minute before she burst out laughing.

"I don't see what's funny," he half yelled.

"I can't stop it. Not without drugs, and Doc and I decided at my last checkup that if I went into labor now it would be fine."

"Fine? Fine? It's not *fine*. The babies aren't due for weeks."

"Dale. I get that you're freaking out. Although with you having worked in law enforcement for as long as you have, I'd think you'd be cooler under pressure or when faced with unexpected circumstances—"

"Tay! You're having the babies early!"

"Yes, it would appear so."

"Early!" Why was she so calm? They were stuck up a mountain, the nearest hospital over an hour away and she was giving birth prematurely. This was not a stay calm or cool moment. "We need to get you to the hospital."

He spun on his heel and left the room only to swing back around and scoop Tatum into his arms. He completely ignored her wet pants. And her protests.

"Dale! Put me down."

"No. We need to get in the car."

"No, we don't. I'm having them at home."

That stopped him in his tracks. "You... Home... *What?*"

"I just need to ring Doc, then I want to get in a bath."

"You want to take a bath? Wouldn't it be better to rinse off in the shower than to take a bath?" He was having problems understanding. Or hearing. Surely he'd heard wrong. She couldn't possibly want—

"Yes. A bath. We're going to try a water birth."

"Water birth..." She wanted to... "Oh hell no. We're having these babies in a hospital where they can monitor every little thing. That's where you have premature babies, Tatum."

Smiling, she patted his cheek. "You're so sweet to worry."

"Sweet? I'd say smart—"

"Dale!" She waited for their gazes to connect and hold. "I'm having these babies in this house and there is nothing to worry about. I've had a textbook pregnancy which bodes well for a smooth labor. Please, put me down. I need to call Doc so she can get over here."

Dale stood there for a moment. He tried to get his panic under control. It wasn't easy but Tatum's calm helped him drag his mental state back from the chaotic swirl it had become.

She didn't appear to be in pain, and he knew what she looked like when she was anxious so he knew she wasn't worried at all in spite of the babies deciding they wanted out early. If anything she looked happy, excited. That alone had his breathing slowing, his muscles relaxing, and his mind calming.

"Okay. Home birth." Turning around he took her back to the bathroom. Placing her on her feet, he asked, "What do you need me to do?" Whatever she wanted—whatever she needed —he'd make it happen.

No matter what he wanted, they were having the babies. Now.

He could do this. He *would* do this.

TATUM LEANED back against the pillows and cradled the precious bundle in her arms closer to her chest. Flynn William Turner had entered the world a full ten minutes before his sister. Caden Rose Turner was currently tucked up in her father's arms.

Seeing the big broody sheriff holding his daughter was worth every second of heartache over the last year. While she'd give anything to have Cade with them, she knew he'd never want to be here, in Whispering Springs, and after being back only a few months, she knew she wouldn't want to raise her children anywhere else.

She was even trying to convince her brother and sister to move back to the mountains after college. Tavia and Tarak had no family in the city and Gramps and Grammy weren't getting any younger. Plus Tatum really wanted her children to know their aunt and uncle, especially seeing how they had the twin thing in common.

Bending forward, she closed her eyes, pressed her nose to the top of Flynn's head, and took a deep breath. As a nurse she'd helped deliver babies and she'd always loved the smell of a newborn. At least with her own children she wouldn't be getting funny looks when she sniffed them. Being a shifter meant scent was an integral part of her nature and living among humans for the last decade, she'd had to resist the urge to smell a lot of things.

The bed beside her dipped and she opened her eyes to find Dale stretched out next to her. Smiling she leaned over and sniffed the little head peeking out of the baby blanket Grammy had made for the babies. She'd made two, of course, and Flynn was snuggled up inside his. Dale had wanted to wait until after they'd cleaned the babies but Tatum wanted her children to be wrapped in the love of family from the very beginning.

It was why she'd made the decision to return to the mountains.

To be closer to her mate, the family she'd been forced to leave behind, and to raise her children among their own kind.

And if she were honest, she'd admit to missing the home where she'd spent the first sixteen years of her life. It saddened her that Cade wasn't with them, that he'd never been happy here, but she knew he'd be happy she was happy, that Dale was happy. And he'd be thrilled to know they'd named their children after him.

Cade Flynn might not have been happy here but he would have been happy for them. He would want them to find their true home. He had only ever wanted her and Dale to be happy.

It would be hard to continue without him beside them but he'd always remain in their hearts. They'd make sure Flynn and Caden knew all about the man they were named for.

He'd live on in their children.

ACKNOWLEDGMENTS

This book was a long time coming. I would love to have returned to the coyote world long before now but circumstances led me down other paths. Finally, almost ten years after the coyotes first found reader hands, they're back.

Over the years people have asked and I've planned, then those plans have fallen through but at last, when I'd lost all hope of writing anything never mind revisiting my beloved coyotes, I'm back in the chair and tapping away. I have the coyotes to thank for that along with the readers who asked when the next book was coming.

I've enjoyed revisiting this world so much, I hope you enjoy this trip back in time with me.

Rhian

ABOUT THE AUTHOR

Rhian Cahill is the alter ego of a former stay-at-home mother of four. With motherly duties rapidly dwindling Rhian is able to make use of the fertile imagination she used to keep herself sane for all those years of slavery. Having spent years living overseas and visiting tropical climates has helped inspire some steamy stories.

Multi-published in erotic romance and contemporary romance, Rhian, with the help of Mr. Muse, spends her days and nights writing.

When not glued to the keyboard you'll find her book or knitting in hand avoiding any and all housework as much as possible.

For more on Rhian –

Website – http://www.rhiancahill.com/
Newsletter signup – http://www.rhiancahill.com/contact/newsletter/
Twitter – https://twitter.com/RhianCahill
FaceBook – https://www.facebook.com/RhianCahillAuthor
Instagram – http://instagram.com/rhiancahill/
BookBub – https://www.bookbub.com/authors/rhian-cahill
Goodreads page - https://www.goodreads.com/rhian_cahill

LOOK FOR THESE TITLES BY RHIAN CAHILL

Doing Logan

Shut Up And Kiss Me

Secret Confessions: Sydney Housewives – Virginia

Boys Of Summer

Bondi Beach Boys

Sand, Surf And Sunnie

Holiday Romances

Christmas Wishes

New Year's Kisses

Valentine's Dates

Secret Santa

Passport To Passion Collection

One Night In Bangkok

Singapore Fling

Coyote Hunger Series

Coyote Home – Book 1

Coyote Wild – Book 2

Coyote Whispers – Book 3

Coyote Law – Book 3.5

Coyote Lies – Book 4

Only You Series

All Of You – Book 1

Party Games Series

Truth Or Dare

Spin The Bottle

Pass The Parcel – Novella

Are You Game Series

7 Minutes In Heaven – Book 1

Catch'n'Kiss – Book 2

Red Light, Green Light – Book 3

Frosty's Snowmen Series

A Touch Of Frost

A Kiss From Kringle

A Taste For Kandy

Hearts Are Wild Series

No More Talking (novella)

Dare You To (novella)

Mad Love

Winter Lake Series

Love Me Like You Do

Love The Way You Are

When You Love Someone

Let me Love You

Wild Rush Of Love

For a full list of Rhian's available books visit her website

http://www.rhiancahill.com/books/